Romancing the Sheriff

Book One
Second Chance Groom

Cheryl Wright

Copyright

Romancing the Sheriff
(Book One, Second Chance Groom)
This is book one of a multi-author series

Copyright 2023 by Cheryl Wright

Cover Artist: Black Widow Books

Editing: Sarah Lamb Writing

All rights reserved. Without limiting the rights under copyright reserved above, no part of this publication may be reproduced, stored in or introduced into a retrieval system, or transmitted, in any form, or by any means (electronic, mechanical, photocopying, recording, or otherwise) without the prior written permission of the copyright owner of this book

Dedication

To Margaret Tanner, my very dear friend and fellow author, for her enduring encouragement and friendship.

To Alan, my husband of over forty-eight years, who has been a relentless supporter of my writing and dreams for many years.

To Virginia McKevitt, cover artist and friend, who always creates the most amazing covers for my books.

To You, my wonderful readers, who encourage me to continue writing these stories. It is such a joy knowing so many of you enjoy reading my stories as much as I love writing them for you.

Table of Contents

Copyright 2

Dedication 3

Table of Contents 4

Chapter One.. 6

Chapter Two 12

Chapter Three... 20

Chapter Four... 26

Chapter Five 33

Chapter Six.. 41

Chapter Seven 47

Chapter Eight.. 53

Chapter Nine 59

Chapter Ten 68

Chapter Eleven 74

Chapter Twelve 80

Chapter Thirteen... 87

Chapter Fourteen 94

Chapter Fifteen... 99

Chapter Sixteen 105
Chapter Eighteen 118
Chapter Nineteen 124
Epilogue 128
From the Author 130
About the Author 131
Links 132

Chapter One

Silverton, Montana – 1880s

Sheriff Sawyer Hicks sat at his desk doing paperwork. It was endless, and he always dreaded the task. He straightened his back and rolled his shoulders. Any wonder his back ached, bending over like this part of each day.

He stood, stretching himself out, and glanced toward the jail cells not far away.

Sawyer studied the sole occupant and his heart pounded. Things couldn't continue the way they were.

"Papa!" His three-year-old daughter Grace jumped up from where she played quietly on the floor, toys surrounding her. It wasn't ideal. He knew it wasn't, but what could he do? "I'm hungry, Papa," she said, her eyes sad.

Sawyer was torn. He'd been transferred to this isolated town several months ago, and was still getting to know the people and the town. So far, he'd been lucky. There had been little in the way of criminal activity, which meant Grace could go to work with him. But that wouldn't always be the case.

"I'm hungry too," he told his daughter, picking her up and hugging her tight. "We should visit the diner. What do you think?"

"Yes!" she shouted, fist pumping the air.

The diner was one of Grace's favorite places in town. Being spoiled and fussed over every time they went there didn't help.

Sawyer put his daughter to the floor. Guilt overwhelmed him, as it did each and every day. He couldn't help the fact his wife had died in childbirth, and had no control when he was transferred from his previous posting. Back there, the townsfolk had rallied around him, taking turns looking after his precious daughter, allowing him to work.

Silverton, his new posting, was a different story altogether. The town was far smaller, which meant fewer residents. Due to there being little criminal activity, he hadn't got to know the people there. By the time the majority were at the diner at night, a place he knew he could mingle, Grace was sound asleep in bed and he couldn't leave her.

Not that he blamed the small girl. No one was to blame, and he knew it to be true.

He reached down and wrapped a hand around his daughter's tiny one, then headed toward the diner, his one and only social outing each day. Being a single parent was a difficulty he was still trying to overcome, but one he'd promised himself to master.

If it meant he had to give up his job as sheriff, so be it. Grace was his priority and always would be.

He opened the door to the diner, and Grace ran ahead of him as she always did, choosing the table she preferred. The table right next to the large window was her favorite. She enjoyed watching everyone walk by, the horses trotting along the street, and well, everything there was to see.

Sawyer knew his daughter was being deprived of a normal childhood, but what could he do—short of resigning his position? Before he could even contemplate such a move, he would need to secure another position. But would they be any better off? Grace would still need to be cared for.

"Horsies," Grace said, then turned to her father. "I love horsies," she said, a smile on her face.

"You do, Gracie," he told her. "I know you do."

The waitress suddenly appeared out of nowhere and handed him a menu. "How are you today, Sheriff?" she asked. Without waiting for an answer, Melody Hammond turned to his daughter. "Hello, Gracie," she said, and chucked the small girl under the chin.

"I'll be back shortly," she said after pouring water for the pair.

Sawyer studied the menu. He'd likely order the usual—steak and vegetables for himself, fish for his daughter. Sometimes he mixed it up, but fish was Gracie's preferred meal. He was far from a decent cook and preferred to go to the diner each day to ensure Gracie ate well. Of course, he needed to keep up his strength to ensure his daughter was well cared for.

He sighed. Something had to change. He simply couldn't continue along these lines.

~*~

As they left the diner, Sawyer decided to visit the mercantile. Harold Jones was busying himself behind the counter. His wife, Helen, stepped toward them when she spotted Grace. "Good afternoon, Grace," she said, kneeling down to his daughter's level.

"We had lunch," Gracie told her, and rubbed her belly. Helen laughed, then stood.

"What can I do for you today, Sheriff?" she asked, her eyes never leaving Gracie. Sawyer knew what she was thinking. *Poor little mite, she needs a mother.* That's what all the women told him. They did it back at his previous posting, and they did it here too whenever the chance arose.

Romancing the Sheriff

He put up a hand to stop her before Helen even had the opportunity. "Please don't say it," he said firmly. "I know, and there's nothing I can do about it." Her nod was almost indecipherable. "I thought Gracie might like a new toy."

Before he could say anymore, Gracie squealed. "Really, Papa?" she asked, then her hands flew to her mouth. His daughter knew exactly where the toys were kept in the store and ran ahead. By the time he reached her, Gracie was rummaging through the dolls and had chosen one. "This one, please?" she pleaded.

One thing Sawyer was incapable of, and that was saying no to his sweet girl. And she knew it.

Gracie held the rag doll to her chest and cradled it as though it were a baby. Which to her, it was, he was certain.

"Would you like a bag for that?" Helen asked, but they both knew what the answer would be.

"No, thank you," Gracie said, and he was proud of her good manners. "We don't put babies in bags," she added, shocking Sawyer. Where did that come from? Gracie lifted her chin in a show of defiance, and Sawyer's heart sank. Was his daughter spoiled? He didn't think so.

Helen leaned toward him, and the words he was dreading came out of her mouth. "She needs a mother," she whispered.

Sawyer knew it was true, but was in no position to do anything about it.

Chapter Two

Elisha Dawson stared out the window of the stagecoach as they approached Silverton. The town seemed isolated, going by what she'd seen so far. There were few trees, but plenty of shrubs jotted about the open plains. She'd been on high alert for the past two days, worried about stagecoach robbers.

The driver assured her it was highly unlikely this far from civilization. She knew he was trying to reassure her, but it only made her shudder. What had she got herself into? How secluded was her new home?

One thing Elisha knew for certain—she would be glad to get off the stage and have a long, hot bath. Her accommodation had been arranged, and funded, for the first two weeks. After that, she was on her own. She only hoped things worked out. If they didn't, she did not know what she would do.

The town suddenly came into view as they rounded the corner. What she could see of it so far was small, and her heart thudded. After her recent broken engagement, Elisha needed to get away. Living in the same town as her former fiancé was not conducive to her well-being. Perhaps even her safety.

Especially after everything that had happened. Much of it still not resolved.

When the letter arrived out of the blue, she was surprised, but it seemed like an offer too good to be true. Elisha had all but forgotten she'd even registered with the agency, and still didn't recall doing so. It must have been a long time ago.

The stagecoach came to a stop. She'd been traveling alone for a few days as the last passenger alighted at Townsend. It had made the journey feel far longer. But now she'd reached her destination, and Elisha breathed an enormous sigh of relief. She waited for the driver to add the steps so she could alight, then stepped off the stagecoach and onto the sidewalk.

She glanced about. No one was there to greet her, nor was anyone heading this way, which she found odd. The final letter, after she'd accepted the post, came with expenses and a ticket to Silverton. She glanced about. Her home town of Tarpin was far bigger than this small town. Elisha wasn't sure what she'd expected, but it wasn't this.

Her luggage was dropped in front of her. "Are you to be collected, Miss?"

The driver's words brought her back to reality, and Elisha sighed. "That was my understanding," she said, confusion in her voice. "I guess I'll find my destination. Thank you for your help," she said, then continued her perusal of her new home.

"I'll move your luggage into the stage office—it will be safe there. You can collect it when you're ready." The man was true to his word, and Elisha felt relieved. Now to find her new employer.

~*~

As she stepped off the sidewalk, having spotted her destination, Elisha took a long, bracing breath. For some reason, one she couldn't fathom, she had a bad feeling about this entire situation. Nonetheless, she carried on, as one would expect her to do.

She had lived in a stagecoach, and out of hotels for the best part of a week, and was ready to settle down. It was likely the reason she had a feeling of foreboding, and for no other reason.

Elisha clutched her reticule and threw open the door. Was this her new employer sitting in front of her? His head had shot up, then he pushed his chair back and stood. "Can I help you, Miss?" he asked, wariness on his face. She had, after all, stormed into his office. Elisha still felt affronted the man hadn't collected her after her long trip.

"Sheriff Hicks?" She would stare him down, as he was doing to her.

"That's me." His expression was still wary.

It confused Elisha. "You do know what time it is, correct?"

He reached for his pocket watch. Her eyes picked up movement behind him. "Oh!" She hurried over to the young girl sitting on the floor, playing with her toys—in a jail cell! "Is this Grace? What sort of monster are you?" she said, clutching the child to her. She stared into the three-year-old's face, then pulled her in for a hug.

The girl's father appeared bewildered. "I…" He stepped toward her. "Who exactly are you?" he asked, then snatched his daughter away from her.

"I'm Elisha Dawson, the nanny you sent for," she said. "And not before time."

~*~

Little Grace, or Gracie as she seemed to prefer, sat on her father's knee. "I hope you haven't traveled too far," Sheriff Hicks told her. "There's been a misunderstanding. I did not send for a nanny." He studied her then, as though sizing her up. Did he think she was a criminal, here to kidnap his daughter?

Elisha's heart thudded. The best thing she could do now was stand her ground. "There is no misunderstanding, no communication error, and I can prove it." She opened her reticule and pulled out the letters she'd received both from the agency and the letter they'd forwarded to her from the sheriff. "Here," she said, shoving the letters toward him. "There's the proof. Do you honestly think I would travel all the way here from Tarpin for no good reason?"

She watched Sheriff Hicks as he studied the letters. When he'd read them all, he studied her. "That is not my writing, and I did not write those letters. I swear," he told her, and Elisha believed him.

Her heart thudded again. "If it wasn't you, then who? All my expenses were paid in advance, including my first two week's wages and accommodation." Tears pooled in her eyes. What was she to do now? She couldn't go back home again. She'd fled for a reason, and refused to return.

Sheriff Hicks stared at her, his arms tightening around his daughter. She smiled at Gracie. None of this was Gracie's fault—she was the innocent victim in all of this. Suddenly, the young girl's arms reached out to her. Her father seemed confused at first, but let his daughter go to her.

Where only moments ago her heart was hollow, suddenly it was filled with joy. The little girl had already captured her heart, which was unfortunate since it was clear to Elisha the sheriff was going to send her back to where she came from.

Only Elisha had no intention of doing that. She had spent nearly a week getting here and traveled in the most uncomfortable conditions she'd ever endured. She had no intention of leaving Silverton until she'd had her long, hot bath. Nor would she leave until she'd completed her two weeks of paid work.

It didn't matter what the sheriff said; she was here to stay until her obligation ran out.

She relished every moment Gracie's arms were wrapped around her. "I love you, Lisha," the little girl said, then leaned her head against Elisha's chest. She rested her head on the child's shoulder and closed her eyes. It's where she stayed until she heard Sheriff Hicks clearing his throat moments later.

"Go play with your toys, Gracie," he told his daughter, and she gave Elisha a last hug, then climbed down off her knee. The moment she was out of sight, he turned to Elisha. "You can't stay. I didn't send for you."

She stared him down. The fact he was almost a foot taller than her did not mean Sawyer Hicks got to tell her what to do. Besides, she'd been paid to do a job, and by gosh, she would do it. "My luggage is at the stage office. When you have time, please take it to the boarding house." Elisha stood. "What time would you like me to start work in the morning?" She tapped the back of the chair, waiting for him to answer.

He seemed confused at this turn of events. "What time do you start work, Sheriff?" she demanded, sounding gruff even to herself. She was tired, dusty, and needed a bath. This man was wearing down her patience.

He frowned. "Er, eight." He scratched his head then.

"I will see you at ten minutes to eight at your cottage." Elisha didn't give him the chance to protest. Instead, she turned on her heels and left the sheriff's office. Once outside, she breathed a huge sigh of relief. Not that she was certain it was warranted. She might have stood her ground with the stubborn man, but that didn't mean he'd allow her to do her job come morning.

Elisha glanced around but couldn't see the women's boarding house. "Excuse me, Ma'am," she said, stopping a woman passing by. "I'm looking for the women's boarding house."

"Down that side street, my dear," the woman said, then hurried on her way.

A fleeting grin had appeared in the corner of the stranger's mouth, but it was gone moments later. It made Elisha wonder if she'd imagined it. Or perhaps this woman was responsible for her being sent to Silverton.

Perhaps there was a conspiracy to acquire a nanny for the sheriff? She mentally shook herself. Why would anyone go to the trouble?

Chapter Three

As the door slammed behind her, Sawyer scratched his head. Then he shook it. What was that about? He knew for certain he didn't send a letter requesting a nanny for Gracie.

Unless he was going crazy, which was always on the cards.

He shook his head again. Now he was thinking like a crazy person. The writing was not his own, yet it seemed familiar. Why was that?

Sawyer lifted his arms and massaged his shoulders. It was clear Elisha Dawson had no intention of listening to him or following his orders. He was still in a daze. Did that really happen only moments ago?

He strode to the window and watched as she crossed the street. She stopped outside for a short time, but he couldn't see what she'd been up to. It was clear, though, she was frustrated. From all accounts, she'd been sent on a wild goose chase. Why anyone would do that to an innocent young woman, he had no idea.

Then it occurred to him. He was the sheriff. A more than capable sheriff. He needed to do some investigations, find out who had enticed the young woman to come to Silverton, and for what purpose. He was perplexed—why would someone, he did not know who, employ a complete stranger to look after Gracie? None of it made sense. He was her father—if arrangements were to be made, he would do it.

He continued to stare until Miss Dawson was out of sight. If it was the last thing he did, Sawyer vowed to get to the bottom of this confusion. He had two weeks until the money ran out and her accommodation expired. Surely he could discover the reason behind all this craziness before then?

"Come on, Gracie," he said a short time later, and held his daughter's hand. "Papa has something he needs to do." They strolled to the women's boarding house, which wasn't too far away.

"Where are we going, Papa?" she said, glancing up at him. As the wind rolled around them, Sawyer noticed his daughter's hair had fallen out of the ponytail he'd put it in this morning. Her hair was a mass of curls—and knots. Perhaps the women of the town were right. Maybe Gracie did need a mother.

Sawyer shook his head. It was the older women of Silverton pushing him to marry. Not that it would be easy—the place was almost devoid of marriageable-aged women.

He suddenly halted. Now he was letting them get inside his head. It would be a cold day in hell when he let a bunch of near-strangers plan his life for him.

"Papa," Gracie said, tugging on his pants leg. "Why did you stop, Papa?"

It was a fair question, but not one Sawyer wished to answer. Instead, he reached down and picked the small child up. "We're going to see Elisha," he told her. Why he was even contemplating having contact with the stranger, he didn't know. He felt an obligation to her, which confused him. He was not the one who enticed her to Silverton under false pretenses, and yet, here she was.

And here he was. Sawyer knocked on the door to the boarding house. Doris Philcott opened the door. "Sheriff Hicks!" she exclaimed, alarm on her face. "Is everything alright?" He shuffled his feet, his daughter still in his arms. "Sweet, Gracie. Come inside, both of you. I'm certain Gracie would like a cookie, wouldn't you, sweetheart?"

Gracie's eyes lit up, and he had no choice but to allow her the treat. "I'd like to speak to Miss Elisha Dawson, if I may," he explained as he put his daughter to the floor. "I need her to look after Gracie while I collect her belongings from the stage office." Was he mistaken, or was that a smirk he saw on Mrs. Philcott's face? Either way, it was gone before he could be certain.

"No need. I can look after Gracie for you. I'm sure you won't be long." She winked at the child, then handed her a sugar-loaded cookie and a glass of milk.

Sawyer frowned. Gracie would be bouncing off the walls by the time he returned if this continued. "If you're sure? I won't be gone long."

"I'm certain. We'll be fine, won't we, little one?" She handed Gracie yet another cookie, and Sawyer groaned inwardly. Why did every woman in this town want to ply his daughter with treats?

"Thank you," he said, then hurried out the door before he witnessed further atrocities that made him groan out loud.

As he hurried toward the stage office, Sawyer reviewed all the information he had. Out of nowhere, Elisha Dawson had received a letter from an agency she didn't recall registering with. She'd been sent money to cover her expenses during her travel, as well as a ticket for the stagecoach. The benefactor had also paid two week's wages and her accommodation for the same period of time.

Sawyer scratched his head. None of it made sense. And how did he come into the picture? Never had he registered for a nanny for his daughter. It was the last thing he'd planned to do. Despite the situation becoming desperate, he would not apply for a stranger to look after his own flesh and blood. Elisha Dawson could be anyone.

Romancing the Sheriff

A child abuser, or even a killer.

Now he was letting his imagination get the better of him. Sawyer quickened his step a little more. He needed to get this over and done with so he could get back to work.

"Luggage for Miss Elisha Dawson," he told the clerk when he arrived.

"Yes, Sir, Sheriff," the clerk told him, then hurried out the back to retrieve Miss Dawson's luggage. He'd expected an enormous trunk, but all he'd been given were two large traveling bags.

He thanked the clerk and made his way back to the boarding house.

~*~

Carrying the bags to room six, Sawyer trudged up the stairs. It wasn't a large house, but it always seemed to be busy. For a small town like Silverton, it was rather surprising.

He knocked on the door. "Miss Dawson?" he called. "I have your bags." He heard movement inside and waited patiently for the door to be opened. It was suddenly flung wide open.

"Sheriff Hicks!" Elisha said breathlessly. "Thank you for doing that." As if she'd given him any choice. "Where's Gracie?" she asked, glancing about.

"In the kitchen with Mrs. Philcott." He rolled his eyes. "I better retrieve her before she is filled to the brim with sugar."

Miss Dawson laughed. "I'm sure she'll survive." He enjoyed her laughter. And her smile. She was a different person now from how she presented earlier.

"It doesn't mean I will survive the rest of the day," he said, then backed away. "I suppose I'll see you in the morning." Sawyer shrugged his shoulders, then hurried down the stairs, not waiting for her to respond. It would be nice not to have to worry about Gracie, and Miss Dawson was easy on the eyes. Perhaps the arrangement wouldn't be so bad after all.

Chapter Four

Elisha watched as Sheriff Hicks hurried down the stairs. There was no doubt in her mind he was a devoted father. She knew little about the small family, except he'd lost his wife during childbirth. According to Mrs. Philcott, Gracie had been lucky to survive. If it hadn't been for the quick thinking of the town's doctor, he may have lost her, too.

Almost the moment he was out of sight, she heard Gracie calling out. Likely happy to see her father again. From what she'd been told, he rarely left her with anyone.

Well, that was about to change. Elisha straightened her back and rolled her shoulders. She had two week's pay that would ensure she stuck around long enough to give him the break he deserved. It was apparent two weeks was not enough, but it might give him a taste of what could be. Elisha might even find herself in permanent employment as a result.

She knew that was wishful thinking. Sheriff Sawyer Hicks was as stubborn as a mule. She'd worked that out almost the moment she entered the sheriff's office. He was unrelenting and wouldn't budge. That much was clear.

She opened the first piece of luggage and hung her best gowns in the closet. If she was to care for Gracie, she needed to look the part. She filled the drawers with her intimate wear.

Then she halted.

Why had she bothered if she would only be here for two weeks? She was almost finished, so might as well keep going now. Besides, she already felt connected to her young charge. Her father, not so much.

Elisha still couldn't recall registering with the agency. She'd talked about it, but did she ever get around to doing it? She scratched her head. Unless she had done so, they would have no way of contacting her. It became more intriguing by the moment.

Now that she'd unpacked completely, Elisha sat on the side of the bed. Today was the beginning of a new life for her. One she had believed to be solid. Now she wasn't so sure. If the sheriff stuck to his current position, she would be on her way again before she knew it.

Where would she go? Elisha would not return to Tarpin, not under any circumstances. These past weeks, enduring the atrocities of her former fiancé, had been beyond cruel. What she had endured was unforgiveable.

Not to mention the gossip that accompanied it all. Small towns—they could be gossip pits. Elisha hoped Silverton was not like that. She would keep to herself, no matter the circumstances. That way, the town gossips would have nothing worthwhile to say about her.

Her attention was pulled away by a knock at the door. "Come in," she called, but the door remained closed. Elisha stood and opened it, and a ray of sunshine filled her. "Gracie!" she exclaimed, surprised to see the little girl standing there.

Glancing down, she spotted Sheriff Hicks. He shrugged his shoulders. "She refused to go until she was allowed to see you," he said.

"Lisha," Gracie said, beaming, then stepped forward and wrapped Elisha's legs in a big hug. This might be her first job as a nanny, but she already knew she was going to love it.

~*~

"Don't be nervous," Doris Philcott told her. "Sheriff Hicks will be grateful for your help." As she finished up her bacon and eggs, Elisha glanced up. She wasn't so sure. "You don't think so?" Doris asked, a frown on her face.

"It's all very curious," Elisha told the older woman, then proceeded to explain the strange circumstances. Taking the last bite of her breakfast,

Elisha could have sworn she saw the remnants of a smirk, but it didn't make sense. What was there to smirk about? She sipped her tea, then stood. "Thank you for a lovely meal. I will freshen up, then be on my way."

Mrs. Philcott drank down the last of her tea. "Have a wonderful first day. Gracie will enjoy it, even if the sheriff doesn't." She turned her back, carrying soiled dishes to the sink, and Elisha left the room without another word.

Crossing the road to the sheriff's cottage five minutes before the agreed time, she watched in horror as Sheriff Hicks led his daughter into the sheriff's office. Had he forgotten she was coming, or was this his way of telling Elisha he still wasn't interested?

She hurried across the road, but didn't arrive until they were inside. This was going to be awkward, she could tell. Elisha stood outside the door and braced herself for the onslaught she expected. She breathed in, then out, then hurried to shove the door open, giving herself the chance to back down. "Good morning," she said before anyone else had a chance to speak.

"Lisha!" Gracie said, then barreled toward her, almost knocking Elisha to the ground.

"Gracie, no!" Sheriff Hicks yelled, then ran forward to stop her fall. His arms went up around her, and

Elisha felt oddly comforted. She felt safe in this man's arms and somehow knew he would not let her fall. "I'm sorry," he said, his eyes proving his sorrow. "Gracie is far too excited about spending the day with you." He smiled then, and she almost melted. Was this really the same man she'd dealt with the day before?

Her hands went around his arms as he brought her back to standing, and Elisha could feel his muscles. If she ever needed someone with strength, she would definitely call on him. She was feeling a little dazed, and he seemed to know it. Sheriff Hicks led her to a chair and helped her into it, then stared down at her. "Don't you ever do that again, Gracie. You could have hurt Miss Dawson."

The child's lips trembled at the admonishment. "I'm alright, Gracie," Elisha told her. "But Papa is correct. I could have been hurt."

"Say sorry, Gracie," the sheriff said, his voice firm.

"I'm sorry," the little girl said, tears now running down her cheeks.

Elisha pulled Gracie into her arms. "It's alright, Gracie, but please, don't do that again." She felt the child nod against her shoulder. She glanced up to see Sheriff Hicks frowning at her. They obviously had differing ideas on how to treat his daughter.

Cheryl Wright

Was this ever going to work? "Right," she said, pushing Gracie away from herself. "What will we do today?" Gracie appeared confused. She glanced up at her father, then back to Elisha. Lastly, she looked toward the jail cell. Elisha's heart broke. This sweet child believed spending her days sitting in a jail cell surrounded by toys was normal. "Perhaps you can show me around Silverton. Do you know your way around, Gracie?"

The girl didn't answer, so her father answered for her. "She knows where the diner and mercantile are, and the sheriff's office. Apart from that, she knows home."

"Why don't we begin with a brisk walk, then we'll work out where to go after that." She smiled at the girl, but Gracie seemed uncertain. "Does that sound alright with you, Sheriff?"

He, too, seemed unsure, but reached into his pocket and handed her a key. "The key to the cottage. It's right next door. Make yourself at home." He smiled tentatively at his daughter. "Gracie knows where everything is."

He didn't seem convinced this was a good idea, but it was only day one. If she was any judge of character, and Elisha believed she was, the sheriff had never spent a day away from his small daughter. It would take some adjustment on both their parts.

Suddenly, he leaped forward and snatched Gracie up into his arms, holding her tight. If she didn't know better, a person would think he wouldn't see her for the next week or more. "Have fun today," he told her, then placed her back on the floor. The girl looked bewildered.

"We will see you later today, Sheriff Hicks." She turned away to open the door.

"Sawyer," he said abruptly. "If we're going to spend time together, you should call me Sawyer."

She stared at him over her shoulder. Was this step one to acceptance?

Elisha admonished herself. Surely the sheriff wouldn't give in so easily. "Then you may call me Elisha."

"Lisha!" Gracie said impatiently. "We going for a walk, Papa!" then edged toward the door again. Soon they were out on the boardwalk, and Elisha breathed a sigh of relief. Sawyer Hicks had relinquished control of his daughter—even if it was only for a day. Now all she had to do was ensure a smooth day of play and fun.

Gracie was a sweet girl. Nothing could go wrong. Could it?

Chapter Five

Sawyer stared at the closed door.

Without Gracie here, the place was silent. Not that she made a lot of noise, because she didn't. Most days she sat quietly on a blanket, surrounded by her dolls and other toys.

In a jail cell.

He knew it was not the best choice for a three-year-old, but he had little choice. His previous posting worked around Gracie. He knew everyone, and they knew him. The townsfolk rallied around him after Lizzie died, taking turns to look after Gracie while he protected their town. It had worked well.

Everything changed when he was unexpectedly transferred to Silverton. It was quiet here, with little criminal activity. He was certain the assumption was he would have more time for Gracie here, but the reality was the townsfolk were unfamiliar to them both. That meant Sawyer didn't feel he could ask for help.

Not that it stopped anyone. The women in town were constantly on his back to get married. To find a mother for Gracie. Even yesterday, at the mercantile, Helen had told him as much.

That gave him pause. Did... He shook himself mentally. How would she even have the means to arrange such a thing? Just because Elisha couldn't recall registering to be a nanny didn't mean it hadn't happened.

He stared at the unlikely pair as they hurried toward the diner. Gracie was apparently eager to show Elisha around. They crossed the road, hand in hand, and Gracie peered through the window. The diner was closed at this time of the day. Probably a good thing, otherwise Elisha would have been dragged through the door by now.

Sawyer turned toward his desk. There was an enormous pile of paperwork for him to do. First, though, he needed coffee. The stove probably needed restocking with wood. He'd not had a chance to do that so far this morning.

His routine had been interrupted. Gracie's routine had been rearranged.

He wasn't certain either of them would get used to it. And then Elisha would go back to wherever she came from.

More than likely, Elisha would be back before he even finished his coffee. His daughter wasn't used to being away from him for any length of time.

Today would be the biggest test, as far as Sawyer could tell. Was Elisha Dawson even up to the challenge?

He glanced at the place Gracie normally sat. He already missed her far more than he ever thought he would. Sawyer shook his head. Paperwork awaited.

~*~

Laughter carried from the street to Sawyer's ears. He'd know that sound anywhere. Hurrying across to the window, he pulled the curtain slightly aside so he couldn't be seen. There they were again—Elisha and Gracie. Wandering along the boardwalk as if they owned the place.

Gracie seemed happier than he'd seen her for a long time. She skipped along in front of her nanny, who was also smiling. He thought they would go to the sheriff's cottage and spend their day there. Not that there was much to do in the cottage. He was woefully aware it was not set up for children.

Lawmen, it was assumed, would not have a family.

His heart thudded. They weren't really a family. Not a whole one anyway. That had changed the day he lost his precious Lizzie. Not once had he blamed Gracie for the loss of his beautiful wife. He was blessed to have his daughter. According to the doctor, she should not have survived.

Sawyer smiled as he watched the pair going about their business. He was truly surprised Gracie had not turned on a tantrum and demanded to see him. Not that she had many tantrums, but she was three. Wasn't that expected at her age?

He suddenly pulled away from the window. They were crossing the road and heading his way. Or more likely, toward the sheriff's cottage. Sawyer had just sat himself back down when the door flew open. "Papa!" Gracie called, then ran to him, embracing him in an enormous hug. "I missed you, Papa," she said, then glanced up at Elisha.

"Did you?" Sawyer asked, warmth filling him. "I missed you, too."

Gracie hugged him again. "We had fun." Now his heart thudded. It had been far too long since his daughter had told him she'd had fun. What sort of father was he to force his only child to play in a jail cell all day? He'd been warned, but didn't listen. Perhaps now he would take steps to ensure her happiness. "I'm hungry, Papa," Gracie told him.

"I'll take her home and make a sandwich," Elisha told him. "Assuming you have supplies?"

"Not a lot. We usually eat at the diner for lunch." The nanny screwed up her face. "It's our main meal of the day," he added gruffly, taking her words as criticism.

"I didn't mean…" Elisha shrugged then. "I'll go to the boarding house and eat. What time would you like me to return?"

She turned away, but Sawyer called her back. "Please join us," he said, knowing Gracie would want it that way. Gracie seemed to have taken to her new nanny quickly. The chance of fun was probably her decider. Not that he blamed her. Children were meant to enjoy themselves, not be burdened by their parent's worries.

"I…if you're sure," Elisha said, concern on her face. Did he think he would demand she pay her own way? Now he was annoyed.

"My treat," he said firmly, then headed toward the door.

Gracie reached for his hand, but Sawyer noticed she also held Elisha's hand. For someone who had only been on the scene for what… half a day, she had become very familiar to his daughter. "I know very little about you," Sawyer said firmly, hoping his tone was enough to coerce Elisha into sharing information about herself.

This entire scenario bothered him. Who was this woman, and where had she come from? She told him she was from Tarpin, a little known town in Montana, but he had no proof that was the case. Perhaps a telegraph to the sheriff there was in order.

Receiving a letter about a job she claimed to know nothing about was also strange.

His unease grew, but Sawyer wasn't sure what to do. Gracie was the happiest he'd seen her in her short life, and Elisha did not seem dangerous. Besides, she had no means to leave town, nor did he expect she would. Perhaps inviting her to lunch had been a good move. They could get to know each other better, and he might have a further insight into the stranger who had arrived in town without notice.

Gracie let go of both their hands and ran ahead. She couldn't reach the door handle, so had to wait for the adults to arrive. "This is a daily outing for us," Sawyer said, adding that it was a treat for his daughter.

"You don't cook?" Elisha asked.

He almost laughed, but forced himself into composure. "I don't cook. We have a light meal at night. Canned food or toast. Sometimes I make bacon and eggs." Elisha's frown made him feel guilty. "As I said before, this is our main meal of the day," he said, feeling even more remorseful. Why, he had no idea.

"If you have the ingredients, I can cook an evening meal for you each day," Elisha told him.

Was she trying to endear herself to him, or was she genuinely concerned for Gracie's welfare? He would probably never know. "That's very kind of you, but…"

Elisha interjected before he could finish the sentence. "I mean it. I'm sure Gracie would enjoy helping me cook, wouldn't you, sweetie?"

His daughter's face lit up, and she clapped her hands. "Can we, Papa? Please?" How could he refuse when it would make her so very happy? After only one day, Sawyer could already see the change in Gracie. Despite all his misgivings about Elisha Dawson, she'd proved herself to be good for the three-year-old. His daughter was beginning to show her true personality. Not the child who sat in a jail cell alone all day, but a little girl who deserved to be happy.

"Sure, why not? After we eat, I'll take you to the mercantile and introduce you. Put everything on my account." He felt like adding something snarky like don't hold back with my money, but realized her services weren't costing him anything. Besides, was he just a tiny bit jealous of Miss Elisha Dawson? She got to spend time with Gracie and with her here, he didn't.

He opened the door and herded them inside. Gracie ran straight to her favorite table. The one next to the window. Sawyer handed Elisha a menu and reiterated his earlier instructions. "I'm paying, and I want you to order whatever you want."

Romancing the Sheriff

"I…" She glanced down at the menu, then frowned. The food here wasn't expensive, but he didn't know what her situation was.

"Please don't argue," he said under his breath. "If it helps, see it as my way of saying thank you for taking good care of my daughter."

She opened her mouth to speak but was interrupted when their waitress arrived. "Melody!" Gracie shouted, then added, "This is Lisha. She's my friend." She had a big smile on her face. As much as Sawyer was suspicious about the entire situation, it was clear Gracie had already fallen in love with Elisha.

When she left at the end of two weeks, Gracie would be heartbroken. And that would never do.

Chapter Six

Sawyer had carried a small box of supplies back to the sheriff's cottage for her, and Elisha was grateful. She could have taken them there herself, but he insisted. Who was she to argue?

The cottage was not large, but it was big enough for the sheriff and his daughter. It was sparsely furnished, as she suspected it would be. It was unusual to see a single father as a sheriff, and Sawyer seemed determined to do both.

She was still fuming at the scene confronting her when she'd first arrived. A three-year-old, or any child for that matter, should not spend their days playing in a jail cell. Mrs. Philcott at the boarding house had told her as much, confirming her own belief. Elisha wanted that to change, hopefully permanently, but if the sheriff refused to continue her employment, she would have no choice.

She stepped over to the wood stove and stirred the thick vegetable soup. Elisha turned when she heard Gracie giggle. "Oh, Gracie," she said, laughter in her voice. "What have you done?" The three-year-old was having far too much fun with the cake mixture. It made Elisha wonder if she'd ever helped bake a cake before.

After cleaning the small girl up from the mixture covering her hands and face, she searched the cupboards for a cake tin, but there was none. Now what? She sat at the kitchen table, which was also covered in flour, and wondered what to do. The mix was ready to be baked, and the oven was nice and hot.

Surely Mrs. Philcott wouldn't mind lending her a cake tin? It was the only option Elisha could come up with at such short notice.

"Come on, Gracie," Elisha said. "Hopefully Mrs. Philcott has a cake tin we can borrow." She was certain the woman would have several cake tins for her boarding house. How else would she feed her boarders the cakes she so freely shared?

She dutifully locked the sheriff's cottage, then headed toward the boarding house, Gracie's hand clasped in hers. Once inside, they headed straight to the kitchen. She could hear the clatter of dishes and other kitchen paraphernalia.

"Mrs. Pill," Gracie called as she ran across the room and hugged the other woman's legs.

"Miss Gracie," Mrs. Philcott said. She seemed surprised to see them both. "Is everything alright, Elisha?" The frown on her face worried Elisha. Did she not think Elisha was capable of looking after her charge?

"We made a cake," Gracie announced before Elisha had a chance to say anything.

"Did you?" Mrs. Philcott appeared surprised at this information.

"We did. But the sheriff doesn't have any cake tins." Elisha sighed then, as though the revelation was only now sinking in.

"Why am I not surprised?" Mrs. Philcott rummaged through a cupboard, then handed Elisha a well-used cake tin. "It's rather battered and bruised, but will do the job perfectly."

"Thank you, Mrs. Philcott," Elisha said as she reached for Gracie's hand.

"You are welcome. And please, call me Doris." She smiled and Elisha felt something shift in her. Mrs. Philcott, Doris, came across as a mother figure. Something Elisha hadn't experienced for a very long time.

"Come along, Gracie," she said, before her emotions ran away with her. "We need to bake this cake before Papa arrives home."

"Cake," Gracie said, and rubbed her tummy. The poor child was deprived. What sort of father was Sawyer Hicks? He came across as a loving father, but it was clear Gracie's childhood was sadly lacking in so many ways.

Well, that was all about to change. Elisha would make sure of it.

~*~

"Papa!" Gracie said as the front door opened. She ran to her father and wrapped her little arms around his legs.

Sawyer glanced up at Elisha. If looks could kill, she would be dead. It was clear to Elisha he still didn't trust her. He picked his daughter up and hugged her tight. "I missed you today," he told his daughter. He sounded genuine, and she was sure he was.

"I missed you too, Papa. Come and see what we made!" She wriggled out of his arms then and ran to the kitchen. "Hurry up," she called to her father. Sawyer hurried to her side.

His eyebrows rose when he spotted the cake on the table. "You made a cake?"

"Can we cut it now, Lisha?" Gracie had been asking to cut it almost since the moment it came out of the oven. "Can we?"

Her face was so innocent, and her patience was at an end. "Of course we can," she told the small girl. Elisha already had two plates ready on the table, but for safety's sake, left the large knife in the drawer until it was required. "Would you like to do the honors?" she asked Sawyer.

He grunted, then reached for the knife. Sawyer carefully cut the cake and placed it on the plates. "We need another plate," he said, looking confused.

"I'll get it," Gracie said, but couldn't reach.

"I wasn't sure if you wanted me to stay once you were home," Elisha told him, truly unsure if he wanted her around when it wasn't necessary.

He studied her then. "I can already see the difference in Gracie. She's obviously had a fun day." He turned away from her then and continued to cut the cake. It wasn't the way Elisha would have cut it, but she'd give him credit for trying.

After the knife was removed from Gracie's reach, they all sat around the kitchen table. "This is delicious," Sawyer said. "I didn't know you were such a splendid cook, Gracie," he said, then chuckled.

"Lisha helped," Gracie said, and the two adults laughed.

After cleaning up the plates and ensuring the kitchen was spotless, Elisha prepared to go home. Back to the boarding house, that was.

"There is soup on the stove, and I've made hot biscuits." They smelled delicious, if she did say so herself. "Gracie has already had a bath, and will be ready for bed once she's eaten."

Sawyer stared at her. "You did all that today, along with baking a cake?"

"Of course. I'm here to make your life easier, and to give Gracie a proper childhood." The latter was really her concern. This arrogant man needed to understand children did not belong in jail cells.

He studied her until Elisha squirmed. Luckily, he hadn't noticed. "Goodnight, Gracie," she said, then squatted down to the child's level. "I will see you tomorrow." She hugged her tight and walked out the door without looking back.

She truly would miss Gracie when her two weeks were up.

Chapter Seven

Checking his pocket watch, Sawyer decided it was time for coffee. He hurried to the cupboard that sat next to the woodstove. "Gracie, would you like a cookie?" he asked. When there was no answer, he glanced at the cell where she usually played. It was only the second day of Elisha caring for Gracie, but how could he forget his daughter wasn't here?

For the past two days, he'd been immersed in catching up on paperwork, and was almost up to date. Sawyer didn't realize how far behind he'd gotten. Not only was he enjoying his job, even the paperwork, but he knew his daughter was having fun. Elisha had turned out to be a godsend, despite his earlier reluctance.

The cloud that had earlier hung over her remained. So far, no answers about the mysterious Miss Dawson had been forthcoming, and that bothered Sawyer. When he pressed her, she shied away, changing the subject every time.

The strange part was, she came across as trustworthy. Gracie had certainly taken to her—like a duck to water. Until he had answers to his questions, Sawyer would remain cautious.

Romancing the Sheriff

Especially where his daughter was concerned. At least being a small town, he could keep eyes on them relatively easy.

The door to the sheriff's office suddenly opened, and he spun around, hoping to see his daughter and her nanny. Instead, the postmaster stood in the doorway. He nodded toward Sawyer. "Morning, Sheriff," he said cordially. "Mail's in."

He took the few steps necessary to reach Sawyer's desk and left a large envelope. In a matter of moments, he was gone again.

Sawyer carried his mug of coffee to his desk, muttering to himself about the number of Wanted Posters he was sure to find inside that enormous envelope. Taking a long draw of coffee, he then sat the mug away from his paperwork. He stared momentarily at the new delivery, then ripped it open.

Sawyer loathed getting new Wanted Posters. Apart from the fact he needed to find somewhere to hang them, he had to study them and ensure he would recognize the criminals should they breach his town.

He flipped through the oversized posters until he came to a Missing Poster. This caught his interest far more than anything he'd ever received before. He studied the photograph and details of the missing person and grunted. What it all meant, Sawyer really didn't know, but he intended to get to the bottom of the situation.

He spent the next half hour removing out-of-date posters and adding the new ones, but he kept coming back to the Missing Person poster. The image wasn't clear, he'd be the first to admit it, but if it was who he thought it was, Sawyer wanted answers. He folded the poster up and placed it in his jacket pocket.

Suddenly he needed to know if Miss Elisha Dawson was even who she said she was.

~*~

"Elisha," he said while they lunched at the diner. "I need to speak with you."

She stared at him, then nodded. "I'm listening, or is it…sensitive?"

Sawyer wasn't sure what came under the banner of sensitive, but he wasn't certain this conversation could be construed that way. "What I really need to do is show you something. Then we should talk." He reached into his jacket and pulled out the folded paper. She watched his every move. "This arrived in the post today. It even has your name below it."

His heart thudded as he waited for an answer. Sawyer hoped and prayed it wasn't Elisha, but the fact they named her was concerning.

She studied the poster, then frowned. "Do I look like I'm missing?" she said gruffly. "Who reported me missing?" She stared at the image that was too fuzzy to make identification easy. "Don't answer that. I know who it was."

Elisha was clearly unhappy, and Sawyer didn't blame her. "When the letter arrived, it was the answer to my prayers. I needed to get away, and I took the opportunity." She carefully folded the paper and handed it back to him.

Sawyer was confused. "You needed to get away?" There was something sinister going on, and he intended to get to the bottom of it.

Elisha glanced across at Gracie, clearly uncomfortable speaking in front of her. Sawyer lifted a hand. "Melody," he called to the waitress, "Would you mind taking Gracie for a few minutes?" The diner was empty apart from the three of them, so he was sure Melody wouldn't mind.

She took Gracie's hand and her empty plate. "Come with me, sweetie. I'm sure I can find some cake for you."

The moment they were out of earshot, Elisha began. "I was engaged to be married. Everything was perfect to begin with. From almost the moment we were engaged, unusual things began to happen. First, my room was broken into at the boarding house. Someone went through my belongings. I must have disturbed them—I heard the window open as I unlocked the door. The sheriff checked it out, but nothing was missing, so shrugged it off."

Sawyer listened carefully but said nothing.

"Then it felt as though I was being watched. The hair on the back of my neck stood up, especially when I was walking home after work. It was usually dusk by then."

She visibly shivered, and Sawyer reached across the table and covered her hand. He could see she had more to say, but appeared reluctant. "What happened next?" he asked, not taking his eyes from her face.

She shuddered, then took a long breath, letting it out slowly. "My room was broken into again. This time they stole my undergarments."

For someone who believed himself to be beyond being shocked, Sawyer balked. "I'm going to assume the town sheriff didn't catch this person. And it's the reason you fled."

Elisha glanced at the table. "I couldn't predict what he would do next. I'm still certain my assumption it was a man is true."

"And you think it was the man you were engaged to." It was a statement, not a question, and they both knew it.

"I'm absolutely convinced of it. When the letter arrived, I took the first stage out of town. If I was honest, although it was curious, it was a welcomed relief."

Sawyer squeezed her hand. It felt nice holding her hand like this. It was meant to be a comfort for Elisha, but he savored it. "I won't report the fact you're here. We'll keep the poster between us two. For now, anyway. I'll have to think about what needs to be done to ensure you're safe."

Hastened footsteps greeted them. "Can we go now?" Gracie asked.

Sawyer ruffled her hair. "We can," he said. When he removed his hand from Elisha's, it felt as though something was suddenly missing.

Chapter Eight

Elisha couldn't believe Joseph had fooled the sheriff into believing she was missing. A quick check at the stage office would have told him she'd purchased a ticket. From the moment all those strange things had occurred, she believed the man was either a fool, or lazy. Even when she made her reports of the circumstances, he didn't fill out any forms.

That was water under the bridge now, and at least Sawyer seemed interested. Concerned even. Did he think Joseph would find her here? She gasped. Would she put Gracie in danger by the mere fact of looking after her?

"Are you alright?" Sawyer asked as they exited the diner. He put a hand to her back to guide her outside, and Elisha enjoyed his intimate touch.

She was warming to him, despite Gracie being forced to play in a jail cell. It had become clear he had no other choice. Elisha had learned more about his situation from Doris Philpott, and it only endeared him to her more. At first, she'd been furious at him, taking away his daughter's childhood. Now she could see he'd done the best he could.

"What if he comes after me? It's Gracie I'm concerned about," she whispered.

"Let me think on it," he said, then followed them back to the sheriff's cottage. Once they were safely inside, he called over his shoulder, "I'll lock the door. Keep it locked." And then he was gone.

In one way, Elisha was glad he was taking it seriously, but wondered if it was all for nothing. Joseph Hancock was apparently spineless. Otherwise, he wouldn't have ransacked her room while she wasn't around. Nor would he have taken her unmentionables. She had since decided the man was unhinged. Otherwise, why would he do such a thing?

She wasn't convinced he would come after her, and could only hope he didn't. If not for any other reason, but to ensure Gracie was safe. Besides, with a lazy sheriff back in Tarpin, there was no way Joseph could discover where she was. At least she hoped he couldn't.

"Can we make a cake?" Gracie asked, pulling her out of her thoughts.

Elisha studied at the small girl standing in front of her. There was no way she would put this sweet child in danger. The best thing she could do now was leave town. It went against the grain since she'd already been paid to stay two whole weeks, but she was certain Sawyer would understand. He wouldn't want his daughter in harm's way, either.

"Yes, sweetheart," she said, far more cheerfully than she felt. "What sort of cake will we make today?"

~*~

"It's only me," Sawyer called from the front door as he came inside. "It sure smells good in here."

"Papa!" Gracie said as she flew into his arms. Elisha watched as he crouched on the floor to hug his daughter.

"You're home early," Elisha told him. "Should I go? The stew will be ready in about an hour, but will need to be stirred from time to time."

She collected her reticule, but Sawyer stopped her. "You need to stay here. My deputy is covering for me, and I'll be by your side until we find the man who has been harassing you." He studied her then, and Elisha knew he was waiting for a response. Not only was it inappropriate for her to stay here, it would ruin her reputation.

"I can't stay here. Not at night, anyway. People will talk." He frowned. Had he not thought through the ramifications? "Besides, I don't believe Joseph is dangerous."

"Perhaps not," Sawyer told her. "He sounds unhinged, which means we can't be certain how he will behave. It's a risk I am not prepared to take—for Gracie's sake."

Sawyer was right. Of course he was. Gracie was his number one priority and was Elisha's as well. She really had little choice but to go along with whatever he suggested. "I'll need to get my belongings," Elisha said, sounding defeated even to herself.

"No need. I've already asked Mrs. Philcott to pack them up and bring them here." Sawyer smiled then, as though he'd done a good deed. And perhaps in his eyes, he had. But to Elisha, it had put her in a precarious situation. One that would most definitely ruin her reputation.

In this town, at least. When she moved on, no one would know her, and her reputation in Silverton would not follow.

"You'll have to bunk in with Gracie, I'm afraid," Sawyer explained. "It's a two-bedroom cottage, and the only other bed is mine."

Her heart fluttered. Sawyer was a good-looking man. If she was honest with herself, he was incredibly handsome. But they were not married, nor would they ever be. She found him quite irritating at times. Like right now, when he was ordering her about and not giving Elisha any choices about what she wanted to do.

Joseph had been like that, but was far more controlling. He bossed her about all the time. In the end, Elisha had enough and broke off the engagement. It was then the harassment began. She'd always suspected it was her former fiancé, but there was no evidence, and the sheriff was far too lazy to investigate it properly.

"Tell me about Joseph Hancock," Sawyer said as she gathered up the ingredients for biscuits. "I need to know everything about him."

Elisha turned to face him. "I've told you most of it."

Sawyer raised his eyebrows. "But not everything?"

A sigh escaped her lips before she had time to halt it. As she mixed the flour and milk, Elisha told Sawyer far more about her life in Tarpin than she'd intended. Joseph had even controlled how she spent her money. The money she earned. It got to a point she took her wages straight to the bank before Joseph told her how to spend it. He wanted to choose her clothes, the food she ate, everything.

Sawyer listened carefully as he drank down the coffee Elisha had made for him. It was far more than Sheriff Dodd had done when all this happened. "The last straw was when Joseph tried to withdraw my savings from the bank."

She heard Sawyer's intake of breath. "Thankfully, the bank manager refused him," Elisha added.

"As he should," Sawyer said thoughtfully. "He doesn't sound dangerous, but we still need to be prepared for anything."

After flouring the board, Elisha rolled the biscuit mixture to the perfect height. She cut them into circles and added them to a floured tray. The oven was ready—she'd taken out the cake sometime earlier. It was cool and ready to eat.

She added the biscuits to the oven and turned the cake out of the tin. She really should get Sawyer to buy one of his own so she could return Mrs. Philcott's tin to her. Then again, she would only be here another week or so.

Elisha shrugged. All of this seemed pointless. If she left Silverton, all of this would go away. Gracie would be safe, and Sawyer wouldn't have to worry about his daughter. Or her, for that matter.

Yes, that was the perfect solution. Her luggage was being packed up and brought here, which would save her a substantial amount of time. Elisha now had a plan and only needed to carry it out.

Chapter Nine

Sawyer watched Elisha over his mug of coffee. It was nice to have a woman in his kitchen again. The aroma of food cooking had drawn him in, but Sawyer knew it was more than that. He was enamored with her.

Gracie adored her, and despite their initial dislike of each other, Sawyer believed he and Elisha were finally on the same page. Especially when it came to Gracie. Not that she'd said it out loud, but Elisha had been right about Gracie playing in the jail cell. It was certainly no place for a child. But what choice did he have?

His eyes watched her every move. The wiggle of her hips set his heart alight. And that smile—his heart fluttered every time she looked at him. Gracie was in love with her nanny, and if he was honest, Sawyer was sure he was falling for her too.

It was just too bad Elisha didn't return his feelings.

Not that it was an option. Sawyer's responsibilities lay with Gracie and his job. Besides, Elisha would leave as soon as this nonsense with her former fiancé was sorted out. At least, that seemed to be her plan.

"Cake?" He glanced up when Elisha held a plate of cake to him. Freshly baked and likely still warm. Just the way he liked it. She was an excellent cook, and that was also a plus.

"Thanks," he said, then tucked in. Elisha grinned as she watched him.

"Hungry, are we?" she said, then laughed. "Then again, men are always hungry," she said and shrugged her shoulders.

He stared up at her. "I'm always hungry when it comes to good food. You're an excellent cook." Sawyer shoveled another mouthful of the chocolate cake into his mouth and savored every bite. "Perhaps we should talk about you staying on after the two weeks." He surprised himself at his offer, but knew it was what Gracie needed. He'd never seen her happier, and it was certainly making his life easier.

If he wasn't a sheriff, Sawyer wasn't sure what he would do. He had to work. There was no choice about that, but he'd been a lawman for as long as he could remember.

Elisha stared at him, then blinked. "I…I'll have to think about it," she said firmly. When she arrived, Sawyer was certain she wanted to make this permanent. He had no doubt the Missing Person posted spooked her.

"If this is because of that poster…"

She shook her head before he could finish. "No. At least I don't think it is." Elisha seemed confused about her reason for refusing his offer. Well, she didn't exactly refuse it, nor was she overwhelmed with happiness about it.

"I understand," he said, when he truly didn't. "Give it some thought. Let me know when you've decided." Sawyer's heart sank. It was clear Elisha had no desire to stay on. He was certain she had connected with Gracie. How was he going to tell his daughter Elisha was leaving?

~*~

"That was delicious," Sawyer said, pushing his empty plate away from himself. "I haven't had chicken pot pie for a very long time."

Gracie rubbed her belly. "It was yummy."

Elisha leaned over and wiped his daughter's mouth with a napkin. If there was a mess to be made, Gracie would do it. He almost laughed, but knew he would have to explain himself.

"Are you certain this is a good idea?" Elisha asked, and he automatically understood she meant about her sleeping here.

Romancing the Sheriff

Sawyer picked up the cloth napkin from his lap and wiped his lips. She watched his every move. "Definitely. I need to ensure you are safe."

She nodded, then cleared away the soiled dishes. When she returned, Elisha served rice pudding.

"Dessert?" Sawyer said with surprise. "Now you're spoiling us." He reached for the bowl and his fingers brushed Elisha's. A thrill went up his arm.

Her eyes opened wide in surprise, and Sawyer was certain she'd felt it too. Perhaps she was right. Maybe she shouldn't sleep here, but it was too late to turn back. The arrangements had already been made. Her room at the boarding house had been put on hold—for now—and her belongings were sitting in Gracie's room.

Sawyer wasn't certain how he would keep his distance over however long it took to catch the man stalking her. He straightened his back—he was capable of anything he put his mind to. Sawyer was, after all, a lawman. He was disciplined and respected women.

It was an unfortunate turn of events that he was falling for his daughter's nanny.

They finished eating, and Elisha started washing the dishes after having put Gracie to bed. Sawyer reached for a kitchen towel and began to dry them. "No need for you to do that," she told him.

"I don't mind. Besides, it gives me something to do." He dried one dish and put it away. Then repeated the process.

Her hand came down over his, and Sawyer shivered. "Put them all in one pile, then we'll put them away at the end." She raised her eyebrows at him as if saying it's common sense. He could see that now.

"I can do that," he said, but what he really wanted to do was pull her close and simply hold her. He wanted to hug her tight until all her troubles melted away, but Sawyer knew he couldn't. They were stuck with each other until this was over. Then Elisha would be on her way to goodness knew where.

~*~

Sleep had been fleeting. With one ear listening for intruders, he had been on high alert most of the night. Sawyer realized he had been foolish to offer this arrangement. Already it was clear it wasn't going to work.

He sat at the kitchen table drinking almost cold coffee, and was preparing to make a fresh cup when his head shot up. Elisha stood in the doorway wearing her nightgown and robe. Her hair was messed, and she was still half asleep. She sent him a tentative smile and his heart fluttered.

She had never looked so beautiful.

Sawyer shook himself mentally. What on earth was wrong with him? He was Elisha's protector, nothing more, and he should remember that. His role in this entire scenario was to ensure she did not become a victim of this man who had clearly targeted her. From what Elisha had told him, Joseph Hancock was obsessed with her. It wasn't something that would simply disappear because she was no longer around.

The only way to stop a man like that was to put him behind bars. That was exactly what Sawyer intended to do. First, though, he had to lay eyes on the man and catch him in the act. Otherwise, it would be considered hearsay. Although he did break into her room on more than one occasion. Not that Sheriff Dodd had investigated enough to prove it.

"Good morning." Elisha's voice sounded different. Husky. Enticing.

He closed his eyes against the picture his mind was forming. Elisha, wrapped in his arms sounded perfect to him. Except Sawyer knew it could never happen. She wasn't about to form a relationship with him when another man was actively pursuing her for his own gain.

"Morning," he said, then offered her coffee. "I was about to refill this one," he said, pushing his chair back from the table, pretending absolutely nothing was distracting him. Especially not Elisha.

He pulled a mug down from the cupboard and made her a cup of tea—her preferred brew, he'd quickly discovered—then made himself a fresh coffee.

She reached for the tea and their hands brushed. He glanced down and as he lifted his eyes, noticed her staring into his face. "Gracie is still sound asleep," she told him. "I thought she might wake when I got up. Thankfully, she didn't."

He didn't want to answer. The image of Elisha asleep in bed was distracting him, so he nodded, then turned away. An idea was forming in his mind, one of many that had flittered across his addled brain this morning.

Before Elisha Dawson had come on the scene, Sawyer was happy with it being him and Gracie.

Well, not blissfully happy. Life was definitely challenging trying to work with a three-year-old in tow. Still, he managed. Kind of.

Now, with Elisha in his life, his entire world had been turned upside down. Not only did he have to worry about her safety, but his daughter's safety was also at stake. Not to mention his heart had already taken a pounding. Had it really only been around a week since Elisha Dawson had forced her way into his heart?

Romancing the Sheriff

He stared into her eyes. They were big and brown. Like puppy dog eyes. Sawyer knew he had to pull his gaze away. Otherwise, he'd be lost to her. Thinking about it and doing it were two different things, and he couldn't think of anything else.

Finally, Elisha spun around and sat at the table opposite where he'd sat earlier. "How did you sleep?" she asked, her voice still husky with slumber.

He sipped his now hot coffee before he answered. "Not well. What about you?"

She quirked an eyebrow. "Not good at all. Gracie rolls around in bed a lot. I ended up sleeping with her pulled close and an arm around her."

Sawyer knew where his mind would go and took a long draw on his coffee. Then he nodded, but didn't trust himself to speak.

"What would you like for breakfast?" Elisha asked, then headed to his small pantry. He assumed she was checking out his supplies. When she returned, her hands were full of ingredients. "Will pancakes suffice?"

"Pancakes would be wonderful. I usually skip breakfast and have coffee."

Her eyes opened in astonishment. "Not anymore," she said firmly, then reached for a bowl in an overhead cupboard, but couldn't quite get it.

Sawyer stood behind her and pulled it down, placing the bowl on the kitchen counter in front of her. The feel of her body against his was enticing, and he truly wanted to pull her tight.

He resisted the urge.

Whether the fact Elisha was in danger was his enticement, or something else entirely, he wasn't sure. What Sawyer knew was he needed to keep his distance. How he would do that with her in the cottage, he did not know.

Chapter Ten

What just happened? Elisha closed her eyes briefly as she added milk to the other pancake ingredients. This was a bad idea. She knew it from the moment Sawyer suggested—or should that be demanded—she move in.

Until she fully discussed her situation with Sawyer, she hadn't grasped the full gravity of her position. She'd never seen Joseph as dangerous, but when he'd demanded her life savings from the bank manager, everything changed.

Trevor Hamilton had been a manager at the Tarpin Bank for as long as Elisha could remember. He was an upstanding citizen, and he'd done the right thing by her. However, according to the man himself, Joseph had threatened him when he'd refused to hand over her money.

Joseph opened his jacket to show Mr. Hamilton his Colt, but backed down when shown the other man had his own weapon. The sheriff had been called, but in his usual form, did nothing.

Elisha shuddered.

"Papa!" Gracie called as she ran into her father's arms. She was such a sweet child, and Elisha would miss her when she left Silverton. The mere thought of it sent waves of sadness through her. The truth of the matter was, she needed to earn a living. Although Sawyer had asked her to stay on, Elisha didn't think it was a good idea. Especially now that she'd been forced to live with him. Her reputation was surely ruined. She would look for a town where jobs for nannies were aplenty.

"Elisha is making pancakes." Sawyer's voice sent waves of warmth through her, and Elisha knew for certain she had to leave. Finding herself enamored with the town sheriff was not a good idea, and she knew it. The moment all this was over, she would leave.

Her biggest regret would be losing Gracie. She didn't even want to think about how the girl's life would change for the worse once she was gone. Elisha was certain she would go back to spending her days in the jail cell for play, and it didn't sit well with her.

Perhaps she could take Gracie with her? The moment the thought entered her mind, Elisha dismissed it. That would be kidnapping, and she had no intention of breaking the law.

She took all her frustration out on the bowl of ingredients, stirring so aggressively, they almost went over the side of the bowl. She reached for the frying pan and placed it on the heated stove. After throwing some butter into the pan, she spooned out a quantity of the pancake mixture.

The sizzling of the pancakes distracted her for only moments. Gracie's oohs and aah's were like salve to her ears. The little girl made her heart sing. Elisha's heart thudded. How could she leave town knowing she would leave Gracie behind? Or Sawyer? She had become far too fond of the pair in the short time she'd been here.

Sawyer was initially a thorn in her side, but she'd warmed to him. Keeping his daughter in a jail cell had sent up all sorts of warning bells, but once she'd gotten to know him, and learned of his story, her opinion changed. That didn't mean she agreed with his tactics, but she could now see he had little choice.

She placed the small pancake on a plate for Gracie and passed it over. "There's more coming," she said, then watched the girl's eyes open wide. "Eat up while it's hot." Elisha then turned back to the stove, cooking until there was no batter left.

She took the plate of the fluffy pancakes from the oven and placed them in the center of the table. The anticipation on Sawyer's face was amusing, but she kept her laughter to herself. "Tuck in," she said, then sat opposite him.

"These are yummy," Gracie said, rubbing her little belly. "Lisha's a good cook," she told her father.

He looked amused. "She certainly is. Perhaps we should keep her," he said, then a look of horror crossed his face. "I didn't mean…"

"Yes!" Gracie shouted.

Elisha rolled her eyes. "It doesn't work like that, sweetie. We don't get to keep people against their will." Except it wouldn't be against her will, and Elisha knew it. She might feel a little apprehensive about it now, but for a completely different reason.

Sawyer studied her, his amusement now gone. "I apologize," he said, and appeared to be truly genuine in his remorse. "It was a slip of the tongue." He shrugged his shoulders, which made her think twice. He said he was sorry, but did he really mean it? There was nothing she could do about it, even if he wasn't.

Instead, she took a mouthful of the hot pancakes.

"They are delicious," Sawyer said, his eyes trained on her. "It's nice having you here." He took another mouthful, and Elisha wasn't sure if it was her he enjoyed having there, or the food she was making.

~*~

"You get Gracie sorted, and I'll do the dishes," Sawyer said once they'd finished eating.

Elisha wasn't sure he'd even know how much soap to put in the hot water. Despite that, she took him up on his offer. After three years of trying to dress the squirming child, he probably thought dishes were the best end of the deal. He was probably right.

"What would you like to wear today?" Elisha asked Gracie, then realized it was the worst thing she could have done. The outfit laid out on the bed did not go together, and was far from pretty. The emerald green skirt did not match the purple top, but at least they would not be leaving the cottage. She felt a twinge of guilt about planning her escape from Silverton.

Who would be left behind to teach Gracie about color coordination and matching clothes? Certainly not her. Sawyer needed a wife. More importantly, he needed a mother for Gracie. She wanted it to be her, but that could never happen. It cut through Elisha's heart. She had come to care for the little girl far more than she'd anticipated. If she was honest, she'd come to care for Gracie's father as well. Not that she would ever admit it.

Besides, she would be gone soon. According to Sawyer, the moment Joseph Hancock arrived in town, he would be arrested and jailed. Elisha didn't plan on seeing that happen. As soon as he was incarcerated, she would leave. She would tell no one where she was going, and could start a fresh life where no one knew her.

It was a good plan, but whether her heart would survive was a completely different story.

"I don't want these clothes," Gracie suddenly said. "I want these instead," she said, reaching into her drawer again. At least the new selection went together nicely. She couldn't imagine seeing Gracie in mismatched clothes throughout the entire day.

"That's good," Elisha said before she realized she could set a precedence. If she allowed it today, would it become a regular occurrence? Well, she wouldn't be there to worry about it, so why should she care?

Because you do, a little voice inside her head told her. *You adore this little girl, and won't be able to leave her.*

Elisha knew it to be true. But what about Sawyer? She'd come to adore him, too.

She only had a matter of days left until her contract ran out, but would she be allowed to leave when her time was up? Only time would tell.

Chapter Eleven

Sawyer washed the dishes and wondered what his two girls were up to.

That thought made him stop what he was doing. *His two girls?* Since when had he thought that way? A shudder ran through him, and he stood drying the same plate over and over again.

Elisha had been at the cottage for a few days now, and she was certainly growing on him. Far too much for his liking. So far, her pursuer had not surfaced, so that was a good thing. But how long should he wait? The waiting and wondering was the hardest part of all.

"I think it might be dry," Elisha told him as she entered the room, laughter in her voice. "Are you alright?" She stared at him then, and Sawyer knew he wasn't alright. He wasn't sure if he would ever be alright again.

He glanced at her for mere seconds. The last thing he needed was to alert her to his foolishness. He placed the dry plate on the countertop and reached for another one. "I'm fine. Just thinking."

She nodded, then stepped toward him and picked up another kitchen towel. "Your daughter believes herself to be a princess," Elisha said, laughter in her voice. "What have you been telling her?"

"That's she is a princess," Sawyer said, trying not to feel embarrassed. Didn't all fathers tell their daughter the same thing? He wanted the very best for Gracie, and would do his darndest to make it happen.

Elisha beamed at him. Did that mean she approved? He certainly hoped so. "Nearly all fairytales have a princess, so it's only natural, right?" Sawyer knew he was babbling, but he enjoyed any time spent with Elisha, and wanted to expand it as long as possible. With the possibility of only days left with her, he was determined to make the most of it. Even if it meant discussing fictional royalty.

"It seems like Joseph has given up on me," Elisha said, staring up at him. She licked her lips then, and he watched as she carefully weighed her next words. "I will be fine to leave at the end of the week. My time with Gracie expires then." The smile had left her lips, and her eyes appeared sad. Was she as unhappy about leaving as he knew Gracie would be?

As he knew *he* would be?

"I… I'm not convinced it is safe. These types, they do this sort of thing. They hang back, making you think they are out of the picture, and then bam!" He slapped his hands together, startling Elisha. "I didn't mean to startle you, but I think you get the idea."

All color drained from her face. Sawyer wasn't sure if that was because he'd frightened her or for a completely different reason. "I see," she whispered. He hardly recognized her voice and knew he had scared her with his words.

He finished drying the dishes, then made coffee. Elisha sat quietly at the table until Gracie came running into the kitchen, a book in her hand. "Read a story," she demanded.

After beverages were made, they moved to the sitting room where Sawyer sat Gracie on his lap. He read the story to her, then she climbed across to Elisha. "Read a story," she repeated, handing Elisha the same book.

"What about a different book?" Sawyer asked, trying to save Elisha from boredom.

She smiled at him and took the book from Gracie. Elisha began to read. "Once upon a time, there was a beautiful fairy princess." Gracie squealed and clapped her hands. Elisha laughed. She continued to read the book until Gracie fell asleep on Elisha's shoulder.

Having Elisha there had helped tremendously. His mornings were no longer stressful and frantic, trying to organize Gracie. And his evenings were far more relaxed. Elisha bathed his daughter each night, allowing him time to sit back and relax for a while. He offered to do the dishes as a trade-off. It was one he happily tolerated.

He wasn't sure what would happen once Elisha was gone. His heart thudded. He absolutely knew what would happen. Gracie would go back to being the sad little girl who sat in the jail cell day after day, and he would once again revert to going through the motions. These past days showed him what a family could truly be like, and he wanted to prolong it.

How he could do that, Sawyer wasn't sure.

He leaned over and gently removed Gracie from Elisha's lap. Their faces were so close and he stared into her eyes. Sawyer knew if Gracie hadn't been wedged between them, he would have contemplated kissing Elisha. She stared at him with those sad brown eyes, and he wondered if she was thinking the same thing.

The moment he returned to the sitting room, he sat down again. "She's sound asleep," he said, wondering if he should bring up what could have occurred earlier. He decided to say nothing.

Romancing the Sheriff

"About before," Elisha said quietly, and his heart fluttered. Sawyer knew in his heart he would have kissed her had his daughter not been between them.

Instead of answering, Sawyer reached for the mug of coffee. Or at least what was left of it. He swallowed down the last mouthful. He wasn't sure if he should even respond to Elisha's *'about before'* comment, and instead glanced sideways at her.

She sat quietly, waiting for him to answer. Sawyer stood. He decided to refill his mug with coffee rather than have this conversation. The one they really needed to have. Suddenly Elisha stood, and they were standing only inches apart and facing each other. She must have had the same idea since she held the empty mug in her hand.

He reached out and took it from her. Their hands brushed, and a thrill went up his arm and down his spine. Sawyer couldn't take it anymore. He placed both mugs on the side table and wrapped her in his arms.

She didn't complain, nor did she try to pull away. Elisha relaxed into him, and Sawyer knew they were meant to be together. The problem was, did Elisha know it?

He heard her softly groan, and his lips curled into a smile. It was exactly how he felt. Sawyer knew he could stand here all day like this. Elisha shifted in his arms, and when he glanced at her, she looked up at him. It was as though she was asking *what's next?*

There was only one next step in his opinion, but Sawyer wasn't sure if she would like it. Still, there was only one way to find out. He leaned in and gently kissed her lips.

Elisha didn't pull back, nor did she slap his face. He took that as consent and deepened the kiss.

Chapter Twelve

Elisha sank into Sawyer's warmth. She could stand here all day like this. His kiss was the best thing she'd ever experienced.

When the pounding began, Elisha was certain it was all in her head, but she suddenly understood it wasn't. Sawyer grabbed her shoulders and put her aside, then rushed to the front door. She closely followed behind.

Doris Philcott stood in front of him, her panic clear. "He's here!" she said breathlessly. "There's a stranger in town and he's looking for Elisha."

"What did you tell him?" Sawyer demanded.

Doris frowned. "Nothing. I told him I hadn't seen any strangers."

Elisha's heart pounded. Joseph had found her. After all this time, he was still looking for her. Panic rose up inside her and she felt lightheaded. She needed to run, but was frozen to the place she stood.

"Thank you for letting us know," he told Doris. The older woman spun around and headed back to the boarding house.

Sawyer's hands pushing her further inside helped, but didn't allay her fears. He closed the door and locked it. Elisha was on the verge of collapse. She was now lightheaded, and she knew she was in a state of panic. What if he located her? It would put both Sawyer and Gracie in danger. That was the last thing she wanted.

"I have to leave," she said breathlessly. Sawyer had guided her to a chair. She wasn't sure when.

His hands gripped her, urging her to stay put. "You can't leave," he said firmly, calmness in his voice. "I want you to stay right here. Inside the cottage." He pierced her with his eyes, and Elisha couldn't refuse. "I need you to take care of Gracie. Can you do that?"

His startling blue eyes pierced her all the way to her soul, and Elisha knew making sure Gracie was safe was the only thing she needed to do. It was the most important thing required of her. She nodded and answered in a whisper. "Of course."

"I'll be back soon. I'll lock the door behind me. Don't open it for anyone except me."

Elisha sat glued to the chair. She felt absolutely helpless, but the one thing she could do was ensure Gracie was safe. She crept quietly down the hallway and stood in the doorway to Gracie's room. The child was still sound asleep, which was the best thing that could have happened. Even at three, she needed her afternoon naps. It invigorated her, ready for an afternoon of play.

Despite all the pandemonium going on outside, a smile played on Elisha's lips. How could she leave this sweet child? Or her father? Not to mention this quaint little town? If things didn't work out between her and Sawyer, would she stay here in Silverton? She adored Gracie, but staying close to them would break her heart.

No, she had to do what she originally said and leave once her contract was up. That way, it would be a clean break. Of course, Gracie would be upset about her leaving, but she would get over it. Elisha's heart thudded. She wasn't sure she would ever get over Gracie and her wonderful Papa.

~*~

Elisha sat in the sitting room for what seemed like forever. Then she prepared biscuits for supper. Now that Gracie was awake, they made cookies. Anything to stop her worrying, although it really didn't help.

She checked on the roast chicken she'd had in the oven since this morning and fussed about making sure everything was clean and tidy. It was spotless, but she couldn't stay idle. What was going on outside these walls? She stepped toward a window, but froze as she reached out to pull back the window covering.

What would Sawyer say? More than likely *don't look*. If she could see out there, anyone outside could see her. Her heart pounded so loudly, she barely heard Gracie speaking.

"Where's Papa?" she asked, her face sad.

She squatted down to Gracie's level. "Papa had an errand to run. He shouldn't be long. Why don't you choose a book, and we'll read a story?" She forced a smile on her face, and Gracie smiled back. Little did the child know the danger Elisha had put her father in. Tears swam in her eyes, but she turned away to ensure Gracie didn't witness her distress.

She followed the three-year-old into the sitting room, and quietly groaned when she was handed the same book she'd read earlier. Then she laughed—until tears ran down her face. Was she hysterical? Gracie climbed up onto her lap and wiped the tears away with her fingers. "Don't cry, Lisha," the small girl told her. It was enough to pull Elisha out of her hysteria. For now, anyway.

After composing herself, Elisha began reading. "Once upon a time, there was a fairy princess," she began, then the pair were lost in the story. This time Gracie didn't fall asleep, and she climbed down from Elisha's knee and chose yet another book.

It was going to be a long afternoon.

Elisha startled at the clicking sound of the front door. Gracie jumped down from her knee and ran to the entrance of the small cottage. "Gracie, no!" she called once she realized what she was doing. Was it Sawyer? Or had Joseph found her and broken in?

She'd had no intention of sleeping. She needed to be wide awake for any occurrence. After the sixth book, her eyes had begun to droop. Gracie caressed her cheek and urged her to wake up. It worked for one more book, and then she couldn't stay awake.

Elisha knew the stress of the situation was to blame. "Gracie!" she called again when the little girl didn't return. Her heart pounded at the unknown.

"It's me," Sawyer called, and Elisha let out the breath she hadn't realized she was holding. "There's no sign of him in town." He shook his head. "It's strange. I can't imagine where he went."

He was devious. Elisha knew it firsthand. "He'll be around somewhere. Let me be a decoy and entice him out." As much as she knew it was dangerous, Elisha also knew Sawyer would ensure she was safe.

"Not happening," he said firmly. "You are to stay hidden right here." He was determined—she would give him that.

For now, she would ignore his insistence and check on supper. "Are you hungry?" she asked over her shoulder. "Supper should be ready by now." Elisha pottered around in the kitchen after getting an affirmative. Sawyer was always hungry, so it was really no surprise.

She could hear Gracie reading her books in her baby babble, getting some words right, but making up most of them. Such a sweet child—Elisha couldn't imagine her life without Gracie, even after such a short time.

Then everything went quiet, eerily quiet. Elisha stopped what she was doing and spun around. Sawyer stood in the doorway, silently watching her. "Gracie fell asleep on the floor while she was reading," he said. "I've put her to bed."

Oh. "I'll put a plate of food aside for her," she told him, then turned around and went back to what she was doing.

"We need to talk," he said quietly, his voice almost unrecognizable. "There's something between us. Something magical."

She knew he was right, but Elisha didn't want to acknowledge it. To do so meant she had to admit she was falling in love with Sawyer. For him, though, was it like that, or was this just a fling? As quickly as the thought came to her, it left. Sawyer was not like that. At least not the side of him she'd seen.

Quiet footsteps behind her alerted her to the fact he'd crossed the room. What was he doing? His arms came up and wrapped around her. Her breath whooshed out of her mouth, and Elisha couldn't help but lean into him. "We shouldn't," she whispered. "I... I'm leaving at the end of the week." Her eyes stared up at him, pleading for him to understand.

"You don't have to leave," he said, then claimed her lips.

Elisha was more confused than ever.

Chapter Thirteen

Sawyer knew he shouldn't kiss her and knew it would be a turning point in their relationship. He also understood the mere fact of their proximity for all this time had forced them together.

Perhaps none of it was real. There was a possibility this was all because of Elisha's situation. She was scared and needed comfort. He was right there, and very willing to comfort her.

Her soft groaning brought him back to the task at hand—kissing this very kissable woman. The one he held wrapped in his arms. Elisha relaxed into him, and Sawyer realized he was in trouble. Big trouble. He needed to take a step back and bring common sense back into this relationship.

He stopped kissing her momentarily, then shook himself mentally. It was not what he wanted to do. He enjoyed kissing Elisha. She was the first woman he'd taken any interest in since Gracie's mother had died.

Suddenly, he felt tugging on his pants. Sawyer glanced down and there stood Gracie. "What are you doing to Lisha, Papa?" She rubbed at her little

Romancing the Sheriff

eyes as she stared up at him. They'd been caught, and he didn't know how to explain it.

"I…" He was lost for words.

Elisha chuckled, much to his annoyance. "Papa was giving me a hug. That's alright, isn't it?"

Instead of answering, Gracie reached out for a hug as well. Sawyer leaned down and picked her up, then all three hugged together. Sawyer liked that. It felt… special. It was not something he'd ever done before, but he'd like to do it far more often.

But that could only happen if he could convince Elisha to stay permanently.

"That was fun," Elisha said, as she smiled up at him. "But now I have to finish supper."

All good things had to come to an end, and this was the end of the hug that had meant so much to him. It made Sawyer wonder if Elisha had felt that way, too.

"I hungry," Gracie suddenly said, and it made him laugh. He heard a soft chuckle from Elisha as well.

"Supper is almost ready," Elisha told her. "Perhaps Papa can help you wash your hands." She raised her eyebrows at him, and Sawyer took the hint. He took Gracie by the hand and headed toward the bathroom. Warmth flooded him as they walked together down the small hallway. Was this what it would be like if Elisha married him and they became a real family?

That thought almost knocked him off his feet. It was the first time he'd had any thought of marrying again. He'd always thought of Lizzie as his soulmate and never had thoughts of marrying anyone else. When Elisha arrived on the scene, all of that changed.

The entire time he spent washing Gracie's hands, Sawyer was stunned. Thoughts of remarrying had never been on his agenda. Why had it suddenly surfaced now? Of course, he knew the answer—he'd met someone he had feelings about. Elisha was nothing like Lizzie. In fact, she was the complete opposite. Lizzie didn't like to bake, and he couldn't recall even one time she'd stood her ground with him.

Elisha seemed to enjoy cooking, and she certainly didn't let him get away with anything. He'd learned that almost the moment they'd met. She didn't hold back when it came to placing his daughter in a jail cell to play.

Sawyer knew he deserved it. She was right to tell him; it opened his eyes further to what he already knew was not good for his daughter's well-being.

As soon as her hands were dry, Gracie reached out for a hug. He wondered if she felt insecure after witnessing Elisha and himself in the kitchen earlier.

Sawyer didn't want his relationship with Gracie's nanny affecting his daughter. Not in such a negative way. "Do you like Elisha?" he asked, then wondered why he'd said anything. It was more than a little clear Gracie adored Elisha.

"Love Lisha," she said, a big grin on her face.

Me too, he wanted to say, but decided it was inappropriate. Three-year-olds tended to repeat everything they heard, and he didn't want to risk his admission being told to the wrong person. And that included Elisha. Before he made any such declaration to the subject of his adoration, he needed to be certain it was how he truly felt. Although he was already certain it was the case.

"Supper's ready," Elisha called from the kitchen, and Sawyer winced. The cottage did not have thick walls, although he wasn't convinced she would be heard from outside.

As they arrived back at the kitchen, Elisha was placing plates on the table. The aroma of roast chicken assailed him, and Sawyer was in food heaven. Chicken was one of his most favorite meals. Not that Elisha could know that. The platter she'd added to the center of the table featured the roast chicken in the middle, surrounded by roasted potatoes and carrots, and a small bowl of green beans next to it. There was a jug of gravy nearby.

He hadn't been so spoiled for a very long time. The last time he recalled having a home-cooked roast chicken dinner was when Lizzie was still alive.

Sawyer shook himself mentally. Why did Lizzie keep coming back into his thoughts? Of course, he knew the reason—he was in love with another woman, and he didn't want to tarnish the memory of his wife. Gracie's mother.

Elisha motioned for the pair to sit down, and he placed Gracie on her chair. The one that had a pillow to lift her higher. Then he helped Elisha into her chair, then sat himself down. She reached for his hand, and a thrill went through him. When he checked, she held Gracie's hand as well. He followed suit. Now he felt bad for his reaction—she was preparing to say thanks for their food.

Elisha closed her eyes and said a few words. "Thank you for our bountiful food, Lord, and for bringing us together. Please keep our little family safe. Amen."

Sawyer heard her gasp and knew the reason. Like himself, she considered the three of them a family now. They were family in all but name. Perhaps he needed to do something about that.

~*~

As he sat in the sitting room reading a bedtime story to Gracie, Sawyer pondered his dilemma. Despite

Romancing the Sheriff

the current dangerous situation she was in, he felt it was better to ask Elisha to marry him immediately.

But when?

"And they all lived happily ever after," he said, then closed the book. When he glanced down, Gracie was sound asleep. How long she'd been that way, he may never know. What he knew was she appeared peaceful, as a three-year-old should. Totally without the worries that surrounded her.

His number one priority was to shield his daughter from the evil that threatened the tranquility in her life. Keeping her at the jail with him had been his way of protecting her. It had taken Elisha to open his eyes to the fact, but he now understood it was the truth. If she was with him at all times, nothing bad could befall her.

Except she didn't get to grow up like other children—playing happily with other girls and boys her age. What he should have done was employ one of the town's women to care for Gracie while he worked. He could see that now. Elisha took care of his daughter far better than he had ever done. Gracie had gone from a sad little girl to one who smiled almost the entire day.

But none of that explained why he wanted to marry Elisha. His heart fluttered just thinking about her. He glanced across and noticed she was drifting off to sleep in the chair. He would take Gracie to bed, then wake Elisha.

It seemed his proposal would have to wait for another time.

Chapter Fourteen

Elisha awoke with a start. She opened her eyes in time to see Sawyer's retreating back as he carried Gracie to bed. Poor sweetheart was weary of being kept inside these past days. If she was honest with herself, Elisha was too.

She completely understood Sawyer's reckoning—he didn't want her to be a target for Joseph. Elisha would happily become bait if it meant this entire scenario would be over with. Except Sawyer wouldn't hear of it.

The thing was, she knew Joseph and Sawyer didn't. She knew what he looked like, and could almost predict how he would behave. From his past performance, she believed him capable of anything to get what he wanted. Or should that be who? Meaning Elisha.

The lateness of the evening was ramping up her feelings. She was already afraid of what might occur. Not for herself, but for Gracie. Elisha believed Sawyer was of a similar mindset. Not that she blamed him. His daughter's safety was paramount—for both of them.

Elisha tried to shake the cobwebs out of her mind by shaking her head, then stood. That had been a bad move as it made her lightheaded. Almost falling sideways had not been on her agenda, but she felt Sawyer's arms come up around her, steadying her.

"Steady on," Sawyer said as he held her. "Are you alright?"

She glanced up at him, feeling more embarrassed than anything. "I stood too quickly, that's all. I'm fine now." Despite her words, he gripped her firmly. "You can let me go now," she whispered, her heart fluttering.

Sawyer glanced down at her, his eyes studying her face. "What if I don't want to," he whispered back.

Elisha knew where this was going and wasn't exactly against the idea. However, she was alert enough to know it was only temporary. For Sawyer, at least. What happened when she went back to the boarding house, and they weren't in such close proximity? They would no longer be so convenient to each other. Did that mean their feelings for each other would fall away? They'd only known each other a short time—a little over a week. How could they even know what they were feeling?

Instead of letting the little voice in her head command her every move, Elisha relaxed into Sawyer. His arms tightened around her, and Elisha knew she was right where she needed to be. She wasn't sure how long they stood like that, but everything changed when he whispered her name. Elisha stared up at him, and Sawyer leaned down. His lips covered hers and she had no thought of pushing him away.

The calm was interrupted by banging on the door. "Sheriff!"

Sawyer sighed. "It's my deputy," he said. "I need to get this."

Elisha watched as he strode to the front door. Muffled voices carried through to the sitting room, and she wasn't sure what to do. Had the deputy found Joseph? Hopefully, he was now behind bars. It was wishful thinking, and Elisha knew it.

Joseph Hancock was devious. He'd already proven that. Still, having a lazy sheriff back in Tarpin didn't help one iota.

Sawyer hurried back to where she waited in the sitting room. "I have to go. Hancock has been asking all around town about you. Including at the mercantile. They didn't let on they knew who you were."

Elisha felt the color drain from her face, and she suddenly felt lightheaded. Would she never be free of her stalker? "Let me go out there," she said, sounding far more confident than she felt. "I'll act as bait for you to capture him."

"No way!" Sawyer said far too quickly. "Not now and not ever." He stared down into her face, then lifted a hand and caressed her cheek. "Besides, I need you to stay here and look after Gracie. In fact, I'm counting on you." He pulled her close and wrapped her in a warm hug, then suddenly stepped back. "I have to go," he whispered, and was gone before Elisha could say another word.

~*~

It was close to midnight before Sawyer returned. Elisha had nodded off in the chair again, but her eyes suddenly opened when she heard the front door open. It was then she realized she had no weapon. What was she to do if Joseph found her and broke in?

She thought momentarily, but realized she would do anything to protect Gracie, and decided she would go with him without argument. He may not even be aware of the little girl's existence, but if he was, she would protect Gracie with her own life. It was the least she could do for Sawyer. And the three-year-old.

Elisha's heart pounded as she waited to see who came down the hallway. She almost fainted when Sawyer stepped into the sitting room. "I thought you would be in bed by now," he said in a whisper.

"Did you find him?" It was the only thing on her mind, but the moment the words were out, Elisha knew she should have made sure Sawyer and his deputy had not been harmed.

Sawyer stared at her, sadness clouding his face. Instead of answering, he pulled Elisha to him, and held her tight.

Elisha's arms slipped around him and, as tired as she was, knew she could happily stand this way all night. After what seemed like hours, but was really only minutes, he spoke. "We will resume the search in the morning. Rest assured we will find him."

Despite his reassurance, Elisha wasn't convinced. Even in daylight, if Joseph wanted to hide his presence, he would. Little did he know his questions would be reported to the sheriff. Despite living in town for such a short time, she'd already made several good friends.

"Tomorrow there will be three of us. Both my deputies will be on the job. We will leave no stone unturned," he said. Elisha heard the determination in Sawyer's voice and knew if Joseph really was in town, they would find him.

She glanced up and noticed the lines around his eyes. Tiredness and worry combined—all because of her. Elisha reached up and ran a finger down his face. Sawyer's hand covered hers and held tight.

Then he leaned down and kissed her.

Chapter Fifteen

Despite being so tired, Sawyer couldn't sleep.

He was overtired, but also had to be on alert in case Joseph Hancock had worked out where Elisha was staying. If he thought it appropriate, he would set himself up outside her door. He'd placed a chair under the handle of the front door, which would impede any attempt to break in. Still, that wouldn't stop Hancock from smashing a window and getting inside that way.

His heart thudded. Sawyer couldn't bear the thought of anything happening to Elisha. He had grown far too fond of her in the short time they'd known each other. Gracie loved her more than she should, and being honest with himself, Sawyer felt the same. Their lives had been turned upside down since Elisha had forced her way into their lives. He had to admit it was in a good way.

The thought made him smile. She really had given him no choice. It was still a mystery about how she'd come to be appointed Gracie's nanny. Sawyer couldn't believe Elisha would forget she'd registered to become a nanny. Not that he disbelieved her, but someone had purposely deceived her. That also meant both he and Gracie were affected by the trickery. If it was the last thing he did, Sawyer would find out how it all came about.

His eyes grew heavy, and despite his wishes to the contrary, Sawyer soon fell asleep.

Waking with a start, Sawyer jumped out of bed. He ran toward the noise, gun in hand. It wasn't until he entered the kitchen he realized he wore only his drawers. Sleep deprivation would do that to a man.

Elisha spun around to face him before Sawyer could retreat, her eyes open wide in astonishment. Her expression changed from shock to amusement far more quickly than it should have. "Good morning, Sawyer," she said, trying to contain her laughter. Her eyes followed him from his head to his toes. He stared down at himself, and did not want to picture the image she saw—he stood there in his drawers with a gun pointing at her. He sighed. Already Sawyer knew he would never live it down.

"What are you doing, Papa?" a little voice asked, and his heart thudded. As Gracie pushed her way past him into the kitchen, Sawyer hid the gun behind his back.

"I… I'm going to get dressed," he said sternly, and heard the tinkling of Elisha's laughter as he retreated. The sound warmed him, and Sawyer knew he wanted to hear it for the rest of his life.

~*~

A mug of coffee was waiting on the table when he returned to the kitchen, this time fully dressed. Sawyer was too embarrassed to even go there, but knew he had to bite the bullet.

"Did you get any sleep?" Elisha asked. The black circles under her eyes were testament to the lack of sleep she'd had. She strode to the table and placed his breakfast in front of him. Sausages, bacon, eggs, and toast. Sawyer had never eaten so well. "Eat up," she said firmly. "You have a big day ahead of you." Her words held sadness, and he instinctively knew she was worried. About him. And his deputies. She should be far more worried about Joseph Hancock. Sawyer would ensure they put the man behind bars for everything he'd put Elisha through. Sheriff Dodd from her hometown would also be taken to task. If he'd done his job, she wouldn't be in this situation right now.

"Thanks," he said. "Don't worry, we'll get him." Sawyer took a mouthful of food. It was delicious.

"It's not Joseph I'm concerned about," she said as she studied him. "I don't think you understand what he is capable of."

"I'm aware," he said, his eyes not leaving her face, not even for a moment. "Between the three of us, we will do what is required to make you safe again." The horror on Elisha's face alerted him to the fact his words could be interpreted as they would kill her stalker, if that's what it took. "Hopefully he will come quietly," he added, and it seemed to calm her.

She walked back over to the stove and dished out scrambled eggs for Gracie. It was a favorite of his daughter's but Sawyer always seemed to make a mess of them. "Thank you, Lisha," Gracie said. Sawyer was so proud of his daughter. She was always well behaved, despite the difficult circumstances, and her manners never faulted. Gracie took a mouthful of food. "Yummy," she said. Elisha's scrambled eggs even looked better than what he managed. "Better than yours, Papa," she said, filling her mouth again.

He couldn't chastise her. Gracie was only telling the truth, and wasn't what he'd taught her all along? Sawyer glanced up at Elisha. She was trying to hold back her laughter. Annoyance overtook him momentarily, but he knew his daughter was right. His cooking was a hot mess. Elisha had spoiled them both with her excellent cooking skills.

Finally, Elisha sat down at the table with them, bringing her breakfast and a cup of tea with her. She was grinning, and Sawyer knew she was remembering him standing in that doorway naked except for his drawers. Embarrassment overtook him once more. "Alright, just say it," he said, trying to keep the irritation out of his voice.

"Say what?" she asked, pretending to be innocent. The quiver of her lips told him otherwise. It only made him love her more. His heart fluttered, and Sawyer knew he needed to tell Elisha how he felt. He did not believe this was a case of being her protector. It was more than that. His love for her was far more intense than he'd ever felt for Lizzie, and he'd loved her dearly.

It took all his effort not to fall to his knees right now and ask her to marry him. Besides, Sawyer didn't know if that love was reciprocated. She had sought comfort from him, but that is a whole different thing to being in love.

Instead, he finished his breakfast and stood. "I'll freshen up, then I need to go. We have a search to undertake. There's no telling how long it will take."

He kissed Gracie on the cheek and hugged her tight. Then he moved to Elisha. Gracie watched his every move, and Sawyer knew he had to be careful. His daughter was only three and didn't know how to filter her words. If he kissed Elisha in front of her, Gracie might let slip before he was ready for it to be public knowledge.

His heart thudded.

If their relationship ever got that far. What if Elisha kept her promise and left at the end of the week? What would he do then?

Sawyer knew Gracie would be upset. Heartbroken too. Already his heart was shattering with the knowledge Elisha could stroll out of their lives with the next stagecoach arrival. It cut him to the core.

Chapter Sixteen

Elisha paced the sitting room, knowing Sawyer and his deputies were in imminent danger. The mere fact Joseph had broken into her room on more than one occasion worried her. Knowing he had stolen her unmentionables was even worse.

Believing she knew his intentions left her hollow. Elisha had never led Joseph on in that way. They'd begun as friends, and it shocked her when he asked her to marry him. She liked the man, so accepted his proposal.

It was probably the worst decision she'd made in her life so far. She had dodged a bullet when the bank manager refused to give Joseph her savings. Not that her funds were substantial, but she would be worse off financially now, otherwise.

The refusal from the bank manager seemed to rile Joseph. He'd even tried to force her to give him her money. It was then she went to Sheriff Dodd who saw no wrong-doing.

Elisha shook her head. What was wrong with the so-called sheriff back home? Perhaps he was in cahoots

Romancing the Sheriff

with her former fiancé. It was the only feasible answer she could come up with.

She stopped pacing. This was doing no one any good, and Gracie was surely bored. "Why don't we make a pie?" Elisha suddenly asked.

Gracie's face lit up. "I love pie," she said, excitement in her voice, then hurried toward the kitchen. Elisha followed behind, then pulled out all the ingredients they would need. Her plan was to make a cherry pie, something special for Sawyer to show how much she appreciated him. Only there were no cherries in the pantry.

She shouldn't be surprised. Sawyer's pantry had been poorly stocked when she arrived. Elisha had been to the mercantile and ensured all the essentials were there. But cherries weren't really essential, were they? Instead, she reached for the apples that sat on the shelf. They would have to do.

She stirred the thick vegetable soup. It would be ready for lunch, or whenever Sawyer returned. She would put the bread in the oven as soon as it had risen to the required height.

Elisha pulled a chair over to the kitchen counter and helped Gracie up. Her eyes opened wide at the rising bread. "That is bread for lunch," Elisha explained. "It's not quite ready to go in the oven. Now though," she said, pushing a mixing bowl toward the three-year-old, and tying an oversized apron around her. "We need to make pastry for the pie." She handed Gracie a wooden spoon and the little girl's eyes lit up.

As Elisha added each ingredient, Gracie stirred it all in, as Elisha had shown her. The kitchen counter was covered in flour, and so was Gracie. She reached over and wiped the flour from her little face. Gracie glanced up at her and smiled. "Am I a mess?" she asked, and Elisha couldn't help but laugh. When the pair cooked, she often told the girl she was a mess. Gracie melted her heart. How could she leave? She had grown to love Gracie and her father. They seemed to become more like a family every day. The thought left her heart hollow.

She knew she could never leave. It would be the biggest regret of her life. Elisha also knew she couldn't bear to see Sawyer each day, or to leave Gracie without being a part of their family. Perhaps it was better if she made the break after all.

Once all this was over and Joseph was behind bars, she would slip away on the stagecoach, telling no one. It was the only feasible answer. Otherwise, she would live with heartbreak for the rest of her life, watching two people she loved with all her heart, but couldn't have.

~*~

There was a knock at the front door. "It's only me," Sawyer called from the other side.

He'd insisted she set a chair behind the door as he'd done the previous night, so Elisha had to open the door for him.

"Any luck?" Elisha asked when he was inside. Not that she needed to ask to know the answer. His expression showed he felt defeated.

"Not yet. We've turned this town upside down and haven't found him. We're taking a break for lunch and will get back to it soon afterwards," he said. "I have about an hour, then we'll start again." Sawyer pulled out his pocket watch and checked the time.

"Lunch is ready. Sit down and I'll dish it up," she said firmly. A tiny smile played on Sawyer's lips. She was getting bossy, Elisha knew she was. Trouble was, Sawyer didn't always know what was good for him.

"Smells good," he said, before the food even reached the table. After placing a large bowl of soup in front of him, Sawyer reached for her hand. "I missed you," he whispered. She'd missed him, too.

"Did you miss me, Papa?" Gracie's little voice cut through the air. They needed to be more careful. The last thing Elisha wanted was for the small girl to feel excluded.

"Of course I did," he said, and she went running to her Papa. Gracie beamed. Such a sweet child. Elisha knew she would miss them both immensely. She turned away to hide the tears dancing in her eyes, then cut the still warm bread. She reached for the butter, then carried it all to the table.

Trying to avert her face away from the observant eyes of Sawyer, she turned away. He reached for her hand again, and Elisha knew he'd spotted her tear-filled eyes. "What's wrong?" His words were gentle, and it was obvious he cared.

Elisha was about to answer, but couldn't find the words. Instead, she shrugged her shoulders and pulled out of his grip. "Everything," she finally said with her back to him as she stood at the kitchen counter on the other side of the room. She'd had no intention of lying to Sawyer, and this way, she hadn't. She merely left out the details.

Elisha carried a small bowl of soup to the table that she'd put aside to cool. She helped Gracie up onto her chair. Gracie leaned in and began to eat. "We made pie," she told her father.

He glanced across at Elisha, then at his daughter. "Did you? Sounds delicious." Bringing his gaze back to Elisha, he watched her every move. "What kind of pie?"

"Apple!" Gracie squealed. "My favorite."

"And mine," he said, then turned his attentions to Elisha. They'd gotten to know each other so well, he could now read her every mood. And she his.

"This is excellent soup," he said, then reached for her hand.

Chapter Seventeen

Sawyer and his two deputies searched in every nook and cranny. Anywhere they believed a person could hide, they checked. Between the three of them, they'd turned the town upside down. He was scratching his head when Brutus Higgins from the livery came running over. "Sheriff!" he called as he got closer. "One of my horses was stolen last night."

That explained it. Joseph Hancock had means to get out of town and keep himself hidden. Sawyer mentally visualized all the outlying buildings and properties he might take refuge in. One that came to mind was an older hunter's cottage several miles out of town.

"Thank you, Brutus," Sawyer said. "I'll let you know if we locate it."

"It's the old gray," he said, then hurried back to the livery.

"That old deer hunter's cottage?" Deputy Sam Halligan asked.

Sawyer was glad they were on the same page. "It's the one I was thinking about," he said. "Do you have any other thoughts?"

His other deputy, Hank Johnson, added, "What about the old Elroy property? That's still sitting abandoned."

Now they had two possibilities, and it left Sawyer scratching his head. "You both know the area better than I do. What are your thoughts?" He glanced from one man to the other.

"The Elroy property," they said almost in unison.

"It's been empty for a few years now, and is quite rundown. Although the hunter's cottage is closer," Sam said.

"But the Elroy place has more facilities. It is exactly as they left it when Henry Elroy died." Hank seemed adamant, so Sawyer went with his opinion. Not that he discounted Sam's viewpoint, not at all.

"Let's start with the Elroy property and if he's not there, we'll move to our second option." Sawyer could only hope he was doing the right thing.

"We could split up," Sam said.

But Sawyer wasn't taking the risk. "We don't know how dangerous Hancock is. I'm not risking anyone's lives."

"Fair enough," Sam said, then mounted his horse. The others followed suit.

~*~

"There's still a ways to go," Sam said, "so we should water the horses. There's a small stream beyond those trees." He turned his horse in that direction and the others followed.

As their horses took in their fill, the lawman chatted. "How much further?" Sawyer asked. "And what are we up against there?" he asked Hank, since it was his suggestion.

"We will be there in about twenty minutes, maybe a little longer. The property isn't huge—there's a cottage and a barn. I don't recall any other outbuildings."

Sawyer was confused. "Why was it abandoned? I thought family would have claimed it. Or did the bank stake their claim?"

"No family, and no mortgage," Sam told him. "That's the problem. Old man Elroy never married and the lawyer couldn't locate any living family."

Sawyer found that difficult to believe. There had to be some family the place could be handed to. That was a problem for another time. Right now, they had a criminal to catch. "If we're ready, we'll keep moving." The horses lifted their heads, seemingly ready to go, and the three continued on their quest.

"This is it," Hank said as they approached a broken down ranch. There was no sign post with the name of the ranch, nor were their fences marking the boundaries. They had all fallen in a heap after years of neglect.

The three lawmen were in the middle of nowhere, and it had an eerie feeling surrounding it. "He's here, I can feel it," Sawyer said quietly, trying to keep their presence hidden. The cottage wasn't far, and as Hank had said, it urgently needed repair. He couldn't imagine how bad it was inside. Still, it would be ideal for a criminal looking for refuge.

A small well stood out front, and there were plenty of fallen branches for firewood. He suddenly glanced up at the chimney. A small trail of smoke was visible. "He's keeping the fire low to stop from being spotted," Sawyer whispered. "But he's there. I am convinced of it." He tethered his horse to the trees where they hid, then crept toward the cottage. The others followed.

Sawyer motioned for them to split up and cover different parts of the small building. Curtains covered the windows, so it was impossible to see inside, but he could hear movement. Joseph Hancock was unaware of their presence. The element of surprise would be on their side.

Carefully turning the door handle, trying not to make a sound, Sawyer cracked open the front door. When he didn't hear running, he continued to sneak inside the cottage. The smell of dust hit him, along with the familiar smell of wood burning on a fire.

His gun clenched in his hand, Sawyer entered the room. There was no one to be seen.

The aroma of food cooking alerted him to the possibility Hancock could be in the kitchen. He didn't know the layout of the place, but followed the smell. His heart thudded when he spotted Joseph Hancock. Or at least a man he believed to be Hancock. "Turn around slowly," he commanded. "Hands in the air—don't be stupid," he said when the man reached for a pot of boiling water. "You'll be dead before you know what happened."

Hancock slowly turned to face him. "Can I help you, Sheriff?" he asked, a cocky grin on his face. "I'm not harming anyone. Merely cooking my lunch. Care to join me?"

Sawyer seethed. He'd already decided Joseph Hancock was slimy, and the man had just confirmed it. "Bring your hands down slowly and put them behind your back."

That was when Hancock glanced about. No doubt checking if Sawyer was alone, and whether to risk an attempt to take him down. "In the kitchen," he called to his deputies, and the smirk that covered his prisoner's face was suddenly gone. "You are being charged with trespass and horse stealing, as well as several counts of harassment and stalking Elisha Dawson." He stared at Hancock then. "Not to mention attempted robbery."

"I didn't rob anyone," he protested.

Sawyer couldn't believe his ears. "Only because the bank manager thwarted your attempt to withdraw Miss Dawson's funds."

Hancock didn't answer. What Sawyer said was true, and he couldn't dispute it.

The other two men arrived in time for Sawyer to hand the prisoner over. "No doubt we'll find the stolen horse in the barn." He turned to Hancock then. "Horse stealing is a hanging offense. The rest would have landed you in jail for several years, but there's no coming back from this."

Joseph Hancock's eyes opened wide in shock momentarily, then his face went blank. "Elisha loves me and I love her."

"She most definitely doesn't love you. You're unhinged. No normal man behaves in this manner." Sawyer growled, then shoved his prisoner toward Hank. "He's all yours. I don't want to see that grubby little freak again." He stormed out of the room and went into the sitting room where he'd entered. He doused the fire, and once the others were outside, took care of the fire in the kitchen as well.

He glanced about the cottage. Apart from a lot of dust and run down furniture, it could be a wonderful home for someone. He took a moment to check over the rest of the cottage. Four bedrooms sat at the other end of the building. One larger than the others, obviously the master bedroom. With the small acreage that came with the place, it could be a good place for a small family to live. What a pity there was no one to pass it on to.

Satisfied the building was safe from being burned down, he strode outside, locking the door behind him. It had already proven not to keep trespassers out, but why court trouble?

It wasn't long before the four men, along with the stolen horse, were on their way back to Silverton. Sawyer couldn't wait to tell Elisha that Hancock was behind bars and she never needed to feel afraid again.

Chapter Eighteen

Elisha was pacing the floor with worry.

Sawyer and his deputies had been gone for hours. She watched as they rode out of town, and her heart sank. She still wasn't convinced Sawyer understood what they were up against. Joseph was both creepy and devious. The combination was not a good one.

"I hungry," Gracie said, and Elisha admonished herself. Of course, the child was hungry. It was past lunchtime.

"I'll make you a sandwich," she told her as she took Gracie's hand and led her to the kitchen. The kettle was on the stove, and Elisha suddenly craved a cup of tea. She moved the kettle to the hottest part of the stove to get the water boiling.

"Where's Papa?" Gracie asked. "I miss Papa." Tears formed in the little girl's eyes and Elisha pulled her close. This was all her fault. What if something happened to Sawyer? Where would Gracie be then? She wouldn't allow her to be sent to an orphanage, so she would find a way for Gracie to remain with her.

Elisha shook herself mentally. The waiting was making her crazy. Nothing would happen to Sawyer. It couldn't. Her heart was doing all sorts of horrible things, making her feel lightheaded and nauseated.

Suddenly, there was a knock on the door. "It's me," Sawyer called. "Let me in." Relief had her running toward the door. She removed the chair in no time and opened the door wide. "We found him," Sawyer said as he wrapped her in his arms. "Joseph Hancock is in jail and won't be bothering you again."

Her relief was palpable, and Elisha was certain she would faint. Sawyer's powerful arms holding her, and his warmth, kept her upright. A tear rolled down her cheek, and he wiped it away with his fingers.

"Everything is going to be alright," he whispered, and Elisha believed him.

After they'd stood wrapped in each other for what seemed an eternity, Elisha glanced up at Sawyer. "Did he resist?" Her heart pounded. She suddenly gasped. "Were you injured?" she asked before he could answer her first question.

Sawyer chuckled, although Elisha could see nothing funny about the situation. "No one was harmed, not even Hancock. I already knew it, but now I'm positive the man is unhinged. He's convinced you love him."

Elisha couldn't believe her ears. "There was a time I thought I loved him, but I soon realized it was only friendship. It all turned sour quickly." She glanced up at Sawyer. Tiredness still showed on his face. The man needed to rest. "It's different with you," she whispered. "Despite the short time we've known each other, I am in love with you, Sawyer. I can't imagine my life without you and Gracie." She leaned her head against his chest and heard his heart rate kick up. She wasn't sure if he was happy about it, or the thought terrified him.

A hand moved over her back, then gently lifted her chin. "I love you too. Gracie and I haven't been so happy in years. You turned our lives upside down and forced me to see things through your eyes. Especially allowing my precious daughter to spend her days playing in a jail cell." He sighed then. "I'll never forgive myself for that."

Elisha didn't know what to say. She knew Sawyer liked her—a lot—but decided it wasn't serious for him. If she'd thought about it, Elisha would have known better. Sawyer wasn't like that. She reached up and touched his cheek. "Gracie is fine, so don't stress over that. But what do we do about the other part?" He frowned. "The part where we love each other," she said, a smirk on her face.

Sawyer turned his head and called to his daughter. "Gracie, come here, sweetheart," he said, then squatted down to her level. The little girl ran into her Papa's arms. "Would you like Elisha to be your mama?"

Gracie's eyes opened wide, and a grin covered her face. "Yes!" she said excitedly, then hugged Elisha's legs. With her heart pounding, Elisha glanced down at the pair below her. What happened to all her plans of leaving town and making a clean break? She knew in her heart she could never have followed through. She loved them both far too much to cut them out of her life.

Sawyer stared up at her. "I don't have a ring yet, but Elisha Dawson, will you marry us?"

Gracie's eyes were open wide in astonishment, and Sawyer stared at her expectantly. How could she refuse either of them? "Of course I'll marry you," she said before Sawyer changed his mind.

~*~

Sawyer stood at the front of the church, glancing back at Elisha, his eyes never faltering. She ambled down the aisle, Gracie a few steps ahead of her. His daughter threw flower petals along the way, and now and then, Elisha gave her a gentle push to get her moving. As soon as the petals hit the floor, Gracie ducked down and picked them up. Elisha could barely hold in her laughter.

Romancing the Sheriff

They had both known it would be a challenge to include Gracie in their wedding, but it was something they both wanted. She was an important part of their family, and there was no way they would exclude her.

The moment Sawyer asked her to marry him, she moved back to the boarding house. It had always been inappropriate for her to be living under the same roof as an unmarried man, but it had been deemed necessary at the time. Thankfully, though, it was no longer the case, and tonight she would move back in.

The moment Gracie arrived at the front of the church, Gracie ran to her father. Sawyer leaned down and hugged his little girl, then picked her up. They wanted her to be included so much, and this was always part of the plan.

Elisha arrived soon afterwards, and she stood next to her soon-to-be husband and her new little daughter. Tears of happiness formed in her eyes, but she refused to let them fall.

The preacher cleared his throat. "Do you Sawyer Hicks," he glanced at Gracie then. "And Miss Gracie," he said, laughter in his voice, "take Elisha Dawson to be…"

Gracie interrupted him. "I want Lisha to be my mama," she said with a smile on her face. Laughter

Cheryl Wright

came from the congregation who had all come to see their beloved sheriff marry his soulmate.

Sawyer whispered something to Gracie, and they both said "I do," although not quite in unison.

The preacher then turned to Elisha. "Do you Elisha Dawson take Sawyer, and Miss Gracie Hicks, to be your lawfully wedded, er, family?"

He seemed confused, but provided the marriage was legal, Elisha didn't care. "I most certainly do," she said, turning to Gracie and giving her a quick kiss on the cheek.

"I now pronounce you, er, husband, wife, and daughter," he announced with a grin.

It was the most unconventional wedding Elisha had ever seen, but she honestly didn't care. It was exactly what they wanted. The preacher then motioned for them to move to the side for the signing of the register, and Gracie tagged along. She was such a sweet girl, and Elisha loved the three-year-old with all her heart. Not to mention her father.

As they walked back down the aisle and outside, Elisha knew she'd been lucky. Whoever sent her to Silverton knew what they were doing. She wondered if they would ever solve the puzzle.

Chapter Nineteen

Sawyer couldn't be happier. Nearly six weeks after he married his soulmate, and his little girl was ecstatic with her new mama.

Today was judgement day for Joseph Hancock, and after talking to the judge, Sawyer knew hanging was out of the question. Instead, the judge had decided to send him to a lunatic asylum. Probably a far worse outcome than hanging. Especially since he would be there for the rest of his sad life.

These past weeks Sawyer had spent trying to solve the mystery of who sent Elisha to him. Although he'd had his suspicions. It was all beginning to unravel. From what he could tell, the older women of town had put their resources together to fund a nanny and her accommodation. No doubt at a highly discounted price, since Doris Philcott appeared to be one of the co-conspirators.

The biggest piece of the puzzle was how they chose Elisha specifically. But now it was all falling into place. The business that supplied nannies was owned by the Tarpin bank manager's sister. The pair happened to be cousins of Helen Jones from the mercantile in Silverton.

Sawyer smiled as he stared down at his final investigation notes. Without all those busy-body women trying to marry him off, he would never have met Elisha. Gracie would still be playing in a jail cell, and he would be an empty shell of a man.

Finally satisfied, Sawyer stood and pushed back his chair as Melody from the diner entered with a meal for his prisoner. "This could be your last meal," he taunted Hancock, knowing full well it wasn't true. He wanted the man to stew over what he'd done to Elisha, then thought the better of it. "Or not," he added, sliding the food under the bars. He wouldn't risk Melody being grabbed by the unhinged prisoner they knew him to be. "We'll find out in a couple of hours when court is in session," he said, then turned away, glad that chapter in their lives was almost over.

Even though he'd discussed the case with the judge, he couldn't divulge the outcome. It was a highly unusual case, and the judge was sympathetic to the circumstances.

As Melody left, Sam, his deputy, arrived. That meant Sawyer was finished for the day. He had important business to attend to with his family, and that was his priority.

~*~

"Oh Sawyer, it's beautiful," Elisha squealed. Gracie ran from one end of the room to the other. "It's

Romancing the Sheriff

dusty, and needs a bit of work, but I'm sure we can restore it to what would have been its former beauty."

"It doesn't bother you this is where Hancock was hiding out?" He truly worried about that, but it was too good an opportunity to pass up.

"Not at all," Elisha said over her shoulder as she headed into the kitchen. "He wasn't here long, barely long enough to have an impact on the place." She smiled as she glanced in the kitchen, then opened doors and checked the woodstove.

Sawyer watched her every move. Elisha was saying all the right things, and her smile said it all. Gracie was still running from one room to the next, and was clearly in love with the cottage.

"The lawyer finally found a family member, with a lot of help from me. We can buy this place for a fraction of what it's worth. Elroy's family aren't at all interested, and since it's so rundown, it's not worth a lot." Sawyer glanced about. There was a lot to do, but together they should have it in good condition in no time.

"I love this place, Sawyer," Elisha told him. "It's a wonderful place to bring up a family." She studied him then, a strange expression on her face.

Then his mind went into overdrive. "Are you... are we?" Elisha smirked, and he knew it was true. "We're having a baby?"

"A baby? Where's the baby?" Gracie squealed as she glanced around. Then disappointment was on her face.

"How would you like a baby sister or baby brother?" Sawyer asked gently. Gracie's face lit up. "Not yet, but later in the year." He knew that meant nothing to the three-year-old, but it might help explain why the baby wasn't here yet.

"Baby sister," she said firmly, and both Sawyer and Elisha laughed. He pulled Elisha to him and held her tight. Gracie pushed her way in and he lifted her up. Group hugs were the best. He adored his little family, and soon they would grow bigger.

He had a good feeling about this place and wanted to see his family settled here. It wouldn't be long and he would resign as sheriff. He couldn't wait to live the rest of his life with his two girls and their new addition.

Epilogue

Two years later...

Sawyer stood at the small paddock closest to the cottage and glanced around. Never did he envisage his life living on a farm. It might be small, but it had done mighty things.

After resigning his job as sheriff, he'd set about cleaning their new home and restoring it to its former glory. Elisha helped where she could, but he didn't want to risk either her life, or that of their baby, and only allowed her to do menial jobs, like sorting out the kitchen and bedrooms.

Gracie had bloomed here. She enjoyed helping with the garden, and delighted in learning to ride a horse. They'd bought a cow, and although she liked to watch it being milked, it was far too dangerous to allow her to do it herself.

"Sounds like Thomas is awake," Elisha said, interrupting his thoughts. Their boy was growing faster than Sawyer believed possible, and was certain Thomas would one day enjoy riding just as his sister did. Perhaps one day he would take over the farm and earn his living selling vegetables as Sawyer did.

He could see Gracie more as the schoolteacher type. She liked to tell everyone what to do. No matter what, she loved her brother to bits. Right now, though, she rode the pony. He kept a close eye on her, but at almost six-years-old, she was more independent than ever. "Keep hold of the reins," he called to her, and she pursed her lips. Gracie knew what she was doing, he knew, but she liked to prove herself. He took a step forward, knowing it would push her into action.

It had the desired result.

Elisha walked over to him and Thomas put his arms out for his father. "Papa," the little voice said, and warmth flooded Sawyer. He would never tire of spending time with his family, and knew he'd done the right thing buying this property. It was but a small blip on his bank account, and well worth it.

Holding his son, Sawyer felt his emotions building up inside him. He hugged the boy and said a silent prayer of thanks for his wonderful family.

"Sawyer," Elisha said quietly. "I have something to tell you."

The smile on her face was all the confirmation he needed. Their family was about to grow bigger.

From the Author

Thank you so much for reading my book – I hope you enjoyed it.

I would greatly appreciate you leaving a review where you purchased, even if it is only a one-liner. It helps to have my books more visible!

~*~

About the Author

Multi-published, award-winning and bestselling author Cheryl Wright, former secretary, debt collector, account manager, writing coach, and shopping tour hostess, loves reading.

She writes both historical and contemporary western romance, as well as romantic suspense.

She lives in Melbourne, Australia, and is married with two adult children and has six grandchildren. When she's not writing, she can be found in her craft room making greeting cards.

Links

Website: *http://www.cheryl-wright.com/*

Facebook Reader Group:
https://www.facebook.com/groups/cherylwrightauthor/

Join My Newsletter:

https://cheryl-wright.com/newsletter/
(and receive a free book)

Milton Keynes UK
Ingram Content Group UK Ltd.
UKHW010840010224
437095UK00013B/342

9 780645 703375